John Godfrey Saxe

The Masquerade And Other Poems

John Godfrey Saxe

The Masquerade And Other Poems

ISBN/EAN: 9783743382695

Manufactured in Europe, USA, Canada, Australia, Japa

Cover: Foto ©Andreas Hilbeck / pixelio.de

Manufactured and distributed by brebook publishing software (www.brebook.com)

John Godfrey Saxe

The Masquerade And Other Poems

THE MASQUERADE

AND

OTHER POEMS.

BY

JOHN GODFREY SAXE.

BOSTON:
TICKNOR AND FIELDS.
1866.

UNIVERSITY PRESS: WELCH, BIGELOW, & CO.,
CAMBRIDGE.

DEDICATION.

HON. ISAAC F. REDFIELD, LL.D.
(LATE CHIEF JUSTICE OF VERMONT.)

DEAR SIR:—I dedicate this book to you, not merely that it may be graced with the name of one of the most eminent jurists of our country, but that, while I make mention of your private worth and elegant literary culture, I may at the same time inform my readers (*loquor gloriose*) that so estimable a man and so good a judge, as well of literature as of law, is my personal friend, and not ashamed to be my Mæcenas.

Of the first poem in the collection (which I have placed in front chiefly because it is the longest, and furnishes a pleasant title to the volume) the plot was suggested by an incident in real life. The tale of "Miralda" is based on a popular legend, of which an excellent prose version may be found in Ballou's History of Cuba. If, in my rendering of Jean Grasset's comical story of the parrot, I have taken great liberty with the French poem, I trust it will be found to have lost nothing except its prolixity and coarseness. As to the imitations of Béranger (I have not ventured to call them translations) so many clever hands have failed of entire success in the same agreeable endeavor, that I may submit them without apology for their imperfections.

While I am aware, my dear Judge, that, with your severe taste in *belles-lettres*, the faults of the book cannot pass unobserved, I console myself with the reflection that no one will view them more indulgently, or more generously seek for excellencies to excuse them.

I am, dear sir,

Very truly your friend,

JOHN GODFREY SAXE.

ALBANY, N. Y., 1866.

CONTENTS.

SONNETS.

CONTENTS.

EPIGRAMS.

THE MASQUERADE.

Πάρφασις, ἥτ' ἔκλεψε νόον πύκα περ φρονεόντων.
Ηομ. Il. xiv. 217.

THE MASQUERADE.

I.

COUNT FELIX was a man of worth
    By Fashion's strictest definition,
For he had money, manners, birth,
And that most slippery thing on earth
    Which social critics call position.

II.

And yet the Count was seldom gay;
    The rich and noble have their crosses;
And he — as he was wont to say —
Had seen some trouble in his day,
    And met with several serious losses.

III.

Among the rest, he lost his wife,
A very model of a woman,
With every needed virtue rife
To lead a spouse a happy life, —
Such wives (in France) are not uncommon.

IV.

The lady died, and left him sad
And lone, to mourn the best of spouses ;
She left him also — let me add —
One child, and all the wealth she had, —
The rent of half a dozen houses.

V.

I cannot tarry to discuss
The weeping husband's desolation ;
Upon her tomb he wrote it thus : —
" FELIX *infelicissimus!* "
In very touching ostentation.

VI.

Indeed, the Count's behavior earned
  The plaudits of his strict confessor;
His weeds of woe had fairly turned
From black to brown ere he had learned
  To think about his wife's successor.

VII.

And then, indeed, 't was but a thought;
  A sort of sentimental dreaming,
That came at times, and came — to naught,
With all the plans so nicely wrought
  By matrons skilled in marriage-scheming.

VIII.

At last when many years had fled,
  And Father Time, the great physician,
Had soothed his sorrow for the dead,
Count Felix took it in his head
  To change his wearisome condition.

IX.

You think, perhaps, 't was quickly done;
  The Count was still a man of fashion;
Wealth, title, talents, all in one,
Were eloquence to win a nun,
  If nuns could feel a worldly passion.

X.

And yet the Count might well despond,
  Of tying soon the silken tether;
Wise, witty, handsome, faithful, fond,
And twenty — not a year beyond —
  Are charming, — when they come together!

XI.

But more than that, the man required
  A wife to share his whims and fancies;
Admire alone what *he* admired;
Desire, of course, as *he* desired,
  And show it in her very glances.

XII.

Long, long the would-be wooer tried
    To find his precious *ultimatum*, —
All earthly charms in one fair bride;
But still in vain he sought and sighed;
    He could n't manage to get at 'em.

XIII.

In sooth, the Count was one of those
    Who, seeking something superhuman,
Find not the angel they would choose,
And — what is more unlucky — lose
    Their chance to wed a charming woman.

XIV.

The best-matched doves in Hymen's cage
    Were paired in youth's romantic season;
Laugh as you will at passion's rage,
The most unreasonable age
    Is what is called the age of reason.

XV.

In love-affairs, we all have seen,
   The heart is oft the best adviser;
The gray might well consult the " green,"
Cool sixty learn of rash sixteen,
   And go away a deal the wiser.

XVI.

The Count's high hopes began to fade;
   His plans were not at all advancing;
When, lo! — one day his *valet* made
Some mention of a masquerade, —
   " I'll go," said he, — "and see the dancing."

XVII.

" 'T will serve my spirits to arouse;
   And, faith! — I'm getting melancholy.
'T is not the place to seek a spouse,
Where people go to *break* their vows, —
   But then 't will be extremely jolly!"

XVIII.

Count Felix found the crowd immense,
   And, had he been a *censor morum*,
He might have said, without offence,
" Got up regardless of expense,
   And some — regardless of decorum."

XIX.

" Faith! — all the world is here to-night!"
   " Nay," said a merry friend demurely,
" Not quite the whole, — *pardon!* — not quite;
Le Demi-Monde were nearer right,
   And no exaggeration, surely!"

XX.

The revelry ('t was just begun)
   A stoic might have found diverting;
That is, of course, if he was one
Who liked to see a bit of fun,
   And fancied *persiflage* and flirting.

1 *

XXI.

But who can paint that giddy maze?
　Go find the lucky man who handles
A brush to catch, on gala-days,
The whirling, shooting, flashing rays
　Of Catharine-wheels and Roman candles!

XXII.

All sorts of masks that e'er were seen;
　Gay cavaliers and hags of eighty;
Dukes, dwarfs, and " Highnesses " (Serene),
And (that's of course) the Cyprian Queen,
　In gauzes rather *décolletée.*

XXIII.

Lean Carmelites, fat Capuchins,
　Giants half human and half bestial;
Kings, Queens, Magicians, Harlequins,
Greeks, Tartars, Turks, and Mandarins
　More diabolic than " Celestial."

XXIV.

Fair Scripture dames, — Naomi, Ruth,
　　And Hagar, looking quite demented;
The Virtues (all — excepting Truth)
And Magdalens, who were in sooth
　　Just half of what they represented!

XXV.

Fates, Furies, Fairies, — all the best
　　And worst of Fancy's weird creation;
Psyche and Cupid (demi-dressed)
With several Vestals — by request,
　　And solely for that one occasion.

XXVI.

And one, among the motley brood,
　　He saw, who shunned the wanton dances;
A sort of demi-nun, who stood
In ringlets flashing from a hood,
　　And seemed to seek our hero's glances.

XXVII.

The Count, delighted with her air,
    Drew near, the better to behold her;
Her form was slight, her skin was fair,
And maidenhood, you well might swear,
    Breathed from the dimples in her shoulder.

XXVIII.

He spoke; she answered with a grace
    That showed the girl no vulgar heiress;
And, — if the features one may trace
In voices, — hers betrayed a face
    The finest to be found in Paris!

XXIX.

And then such wit! — in repartee
    She shone without the least endeavor;
A beauty and a *bel-esprit!*
A scholar, too, — 't was plain to see, —
    Who ever saw a girl so clever?

XXX.

Her taste he ventured to explore
  In books — the graver and the lighter —
And mentioned authors by the score ;
Mon Dieu ! — in every sort of lore
  She always chose his favorite writer !

XXXI.

She loved the poets ; but confessed
  Racine beat all the others hollow ;
At least, she thought his *style* the best —
(Racine ! *his* literary test !
  Racine ! his *Maximus Apollo !)*

XXXII.

Whatever topic he might name,
  Their minds were strangely sympathetic ;
Of courtship, marriage, fashion, fame,
Their views and feelings were the same, —
  "*Parblieu!*" he cried, "it looks prophetic!"

XXXIII.

" Come, let us seek an ampler space ;
    This heated room — I can't abide it !
That mask, I 'm sure, is out of place,
And hides the fairest, sweetest face — "
    Said she, " I wear the mask to hide it ! "

XXXIV.

The answer was extremely pat,
    And gave the Count a deal of pleasure :
" *C'est vrai !* — I did not think of that !
Come, let us go where we can chat
    And eat (I 'm hungry) at our leisure."

XXXV.

" I 'm hungry too ! " she said, — and went,
    Without the least attempt to cozen, —
Like ladies who refuse, relent,
Debate, oppose, and then consent
    To — eat enough for half a dozen !

XXXVI.

And so they sat them down to dine,
  Solus cum sola, gay and merry ;
The Count inquires the sort of wine
To which his charmer may incline, —
  Ah! quelle merveille! she answers, " Sherry ! "

XXXVII.

What will she eat ? She takes the *carte*,
  And notes the viands that she wishes ;
"*Pardon, Monsieur!* what makes you start?"
As if she knew his tastes by heart,
  The lady named his favorite dishes !

XXXVIII.

Was e'er such sympathy before ?
  The Count was really half demented ;
He kissed her hand, and roundly swore
He loved her perfectly ! — and, more, —
  He 'd wed her — if the gods consented !

XXXIX.

" Monsieur is very kind," she said,

　" His love so lavishly bestowing

On one who never thought to wed, —

And least of all " — she raised her head —

　" 'T is late, Sir Knight, I must be going ! "

XL.

Count Felix sighed, — and while he drew

　Her shawl about her, at his leisure,

" What street ? " he asked ; " my cab is due."

" No ! — no ! " she said, " *I go with you !*

　That is — if it may be your pleasure."

XLI.

Of course, there 's little need to say

　The Count delighted in her capture ;

Away he drove, — and all the way

He murmured, " *Quelle félicité !* "

　In very ecstasy of rapture !

XLII.

Arrived at home — just where a fount
  Shot forth a jet of lucent water —
He helped the lady to dismount;
She drops her mask — and lo ! — the Count —
  Sees — *Dieu de ciel !* — his only daughter !

XLIII.

" Good night ! " she said, — " I 'm very well,
  Although you thought my health was fading;
Be good — and I will never tell
('T was funny though) of what befell
  When you and I went masquerading ! "

WHAT HAS BECOME OF THE GODS.

FULL often I had heard it said,
　　As something quite uncontroverted,
"The gods and goddesses are dead,
　　And high Olympus is deserted ";
And so, while thinking of the gods,
　　I made, one night, an exploration,
(In fact or fancy, — where 's the odds?)
　　To get authentic information.

I found — to make a true report,
　　As if I were a sworn committee —
They all had left the upper court,
　　And settled in Manhattan city;

Where now they live, as best they may,
    Quite unsuspected of their neighbors,
And in a humbler sort of way,
    Repeat their old Olympic labors.

In human frames, for safe disguise,
    They come and go through wooden portals,
And to the keen Detective's eyes
    Seem nothing more than common mortals;
For mortal-like they 're clad and fed,
    And, still to blind the sharp inspector,
Eat, for ambrosia, baker's bread,
    And tipple — everything but nectar.

Great Jove, who wore the kingly crown,
    And used to make Olympus rattle,
As if the sky was coming down,
    Or all the Titans were in battle, —
Is now a sorry playhouse wight,
    Content to make the groundlings wonder,

And earn some shillings every night,
   By coining cheap theatric thunder.

Apollo, who in better times
   Was poet-laureate of th' Elysians,
And, adding medicine to rhymes,
   Was chief among the court physicians,
Now cures disease of every grade, —
   Lucina's cares and *Cupid's* curses, —
And, still to ply his double trade,
   Bepuffs his pills in doggerel verses!

Minerva, famous in her day
   For wit and war, — though often shocking
The gods by overmuch display
   Of what they called her azure stocking, —
Now deals in books of ancient kind,
   (Whose Learning soars and Fancy grovels,)
And, to indulge her warlike mind,
   Writes very sanguinary novels.

And Venus, who on Ida's seat
   In myrtle-groves her charms paraded,
Displays her beauty in the street,
   And seems, indeed, a little faded ;
She 's dealing in the clothing-line,
   (If at her word you choose to take her,)
In *Something Square* you read the sign : —
   "Miss Cytherea, Mantua-Maker."

Mars figures still as god of war,
   But not with spear and iron hanger,
Erect upon the ponderous car
   That rolled along with fearful clangor, —
Ah ! no ; of sword and spear bereft,
   He stands beside his bottle-holder,
And plumps his *right*, and plants his *left*,
   And strikes directly from the shoulder.

And Bacchus, reared among the vines
   That flourished in the fields Elysian,

And ruddy with the rarest wines
  That ever flashed upon the vision, —
A licensed liquor-dealer now,
  Sits pale and thin from over-dosing
With whisky, made — the deuce knows how,
  And brandy of his own composing.

And cunning Mercury, — what d' ye think
  Is now the nimble rogue's condition ?
Of course 't was but a step, to sink
  From *Peter Funk* to politician ;
Though now he neither steals nor robs,
  But just secures a friend's election,
And lives and thrives on little jobs
  Connected with the Street Inspection.

Thus all the gods, in deep disguise,
  Go in and out of wooden portals,
And, to the sharpest human eyes,
  Seem nothing more than common mortals.

And so they live, as best they may,
   Quite unsuspected of their neighbors,
And, in a humbler sort of way,
   Repeat their old Olympic labors.

THE POET'S LICENSE.

THE Poet's License! — Some there are
 Who hold the false opinion
'T is but a meagre privilege
 Confined to Art's dominion;
The right to rhyme quite unrestrained
 By certain rigid fetters
Which bind the colder men of prose,
 Within the realm of letters.

Ah no! — I deem 't is something more,
 And something vastly higher,
To which the proudest bard on earth
 May worthily aspire.

The Poet's License ! — 't is the right,
  Within the rule of duty,
To look on all delightful things
  Throughout the world of beauty.

To gaze with rapture at the stars
  That in the skies are glowing;
To see the gems of perfect dye
  That in the woods are growing, —
And more than sage astronomer,
  And more than learnéd florist,
To read the glorious homilies
  Of Firmament and Forest.

When Nature gives a gorgeous rose,
  Or yields the simplest fern,
She writes this motto on the leaves, —
  " To whom it may concern ! "
And so it is the poet comes
  And revels in her bowers,

2

And, though another hold the land,
 Is owner of the flowers.

O nevermore let Ignorance
 With heedless iteration
Repeat the phrase as meaning aught
 Of trivial estimation ;
The Poet's License ! — 'T is the fee
 Of earth and sky and river
To him who views them royally,
 To have and hold forever !

THE EXPECTED SHIP.

THUS I heard a poet say,
   As he sang in merry glee,
" Ah ! 't will be a golden day,
   When my ship comes o'er the sea !

" I do know a cottage fine,
   As a poet's house should be, ·
And the cottage shall be mine,
   When my ship comes o'er the sea !

" I do know a maiden fair,
   Fair, and fond, and dear to me,
And we 'll be a wedded pair,
   When my ship comes o'er the sea !

" And within that cottage fine,
   Blest as any king may be,
Every pleasure shall be mine,
   When my ship comes o'er the sea!

" To be rich is to be great;
   Love is only for the free;
Grant me patience, while I wait
   Till my ship comes o'er the sea! "

Months and years have come and gone
   Since the poet sang to me,
Yet he still keeps hoping on
   For the ship from o'er the sea!

Thus the siren voice of Hope
   Whispers still to you and me
Of something in the future's scope,
   Some golden ship from o'er the sea!

Never sailor yet hath found,
    Looking windward or to lee,
Any vessel homeward bound,
    Like that ship from o'er the sea !

Never comes the shining deck ;
    But that tiny cloud may be,
Though it seems the merest speck,
    The promised ship from o'er the sea !

Never looms the swelling sail,
    But the wind is blowing free,
And *that* may be the precious gale
    That brings the ship from o'er the sea !

THE STORY OF LIFE.

SAY, what is life? 'T is to be born;
  A helpless *Babe*, to greet the light
With a sharp wail, as if the morn
  Foretold a cloudy noon and night;
To weep, to sleep, and weep again,
With sunny smiles between; and then?

And then apace the infant grows
  To be a laughing, puling boy,
Happy, despite his little woes,
  Were he but conscious of his joy;
To be, in short, from two to ten,
A merry, moody *Child;* and then?

And then, in coat and trousers clad,
 To learn to say the Decalogue,
And break it; an unthinking *Lad*,
 With mirth and mischief all agog;
A truant oft by field and fen
To capture butterflies; and then?

And then, increased in strength and size,
 To be, anon, a *Youth* full-grown;
A hero in his mother's eyes,
 A young Apollo in his own;
To imitate the ways of men
In fashionable sins; and then?

And then, at last, to be a *Man;*
 To fall in love; to woo and wed;
With seething brain to scheme and plan;
 To gather gold, or toil for bread;
To sue for fame with tongue or pen,
And gain or lose the prize; and then?

And then in gray and wrinkled *Eld*
 To mourn the speed of life's decline ;
To praise the scenes his youth beheld,
 And dwell in memory of Lang-Syne ;
To dream awhile with darkened ken,
Then drop into his grave, and then ?

THE GREAT MAGICIAN.

Ecce iterum Figulus ! *

O NCE, when a lad, it was my hap
　　To gain my mother's kind permission
To go and see a foreign chap
　　Who called himself " The Great Magician ";
I recollect his wondrous skill
　　In divers mystic conjurations,
And how the fellow wrought at will
　　The most prodigious transformations.

I recollect the nervous man
　　Within whose hat the great deceiver

* " Potter, the Great Magician," a clever conjurer of a former generation, is still vividly remembered by many people
in New Hampshire and Vermont.

Broke eggs, as in a frying-pan,
　　And took 'em smoking from the beaver !
I recollect the lady's shawl
　　Which the magician rent asunder,
And then restored ; but, best of all,
　　I recollect the Ribbon-Wonder !

I mean, of course, the funny freak
　　In which the wizard, at his pleasure,
Spins lots of ribbons from his cheek,
　.　(Where he had hid 'em, at his leisure,)
Yard after yard, of every hue,
　　Comes blazing out, and still the fellow
Keeps spinning ribbons, red and blue,
　　And black, and white, and green, and yellow !

I ne'er shall see another show
　　To rank with the immortal "Potter's " ;
He 's dead and buried long ago,
　　And others charm our sons and daughters ;

Years — years have fled — alas! how quick,
    Since I beheld the Great Magician,
And yet I 've seen the Ribbon-Trick
    In many a curious repetition!

Thus, when an author I have read
    Who much amazed the world of letters
With gems his fluent pen has shed,
    (All nicely pilfered from his betters,)
Presto! — 't is done! — and all complete,
    As in my youth's enraptured vision,
I 've seen again the Ribbon-Feat,
    And thought about the Great Magician!

So, when a sermon I have heard
    Made up of bits of borrowed learning,
Some cheap mosaic which has stirred
    The wonder of the undiscerning, —
Swift as a flash has memory then
    Recalled the ancient exhibition;

I saw the Ribbon-Trick again,
　　And thought about the Great Magician !

So when some flippant man-o'-jokes,
　　Though in himself no dunce was duller,
Has dazzled all the simple folks
　　With brilliant jests of every color, —
I 've whispered thus (while fast and thick
　　The changes flashed across my vision) : —
" How well he plays the Ribbon-Trick !
　　By Jove ! — he beats the Great Magician ! "

I ne'er shall see another show
　　To rank with the immortal " Potter's " ;
He 's dead and buried long ago,
　　And other wizards take the quarters ;
Years — years have fled — alas ! how quick,
　　Since I beheld the Great Magician,
And yet I 've seen the Ribbon-Trick
　　In many a curious repetition !

THE BLARNEY STONE.

I.

IN Blarney Castle, on a crumbling tower,
   There lies a stone, (above your ready
     reach,)
Which to the lips imparts, 't is said, the power
   Of facile falsehood, and persuasive speech;
And hence, of one who talks in such a tone,
The peasants say, "He 's kissed the Blarney
     Stone!"

II.

Thus, when I see some flippant tourist swell
   With secrets wrested from an Emperor,—

And hear him vaunt his bravery, and tell

How once he snubbed a Marquis, — I infer

The man came back — if but the truth were

known —

By way of Cork, and kissed the Blarney Stone!

III.

So, when I hear a shallow dandy boast

(In the long car that marks a brother dunce)

What precious favors ladies' lips have lost,

To his advantage; I suspect, at once,

The fellow's lying; that the dog alone

(Enough for him!) has kissed the Blarney Stone!

IV.

When some fine lady, — ready to defame

An absent beauty, with as sweet a·grace, —

With seeming rapture greets a hated name,

And lauds her rival to her wondering face;

E'en Charity herself must freely own

Some women, too, have kissed the Blarney

Stone! ·

V.

When sleek attorneys, whose seductive tongues,
  Smooth with the unction of a golden fee,
" Breathe forth huge falsehoods from capacious
     lungs," *
(The words are Juvenal's) 't is plain to see
A lawyer's genius is n't all his own ;
The specious rogue has kissed the Blarney
     Stone !

VI.

When the false pastor, from his fainting flock
  Withholds the Bread of Life — the Gospel
     news —
To give them dainty words, lest he should shock
  The fragile fabric of the paying pews, —
Who but must feel, the man, to Grace unknown,
Has kissed, — not Calvary, — but the Blarney
     Stone !

* " Immensa cavi spirant mendacia folles."

THE MOURNER À LA MODE.

I SAW her last night at a party,
  (The elegant party at Mead's,)
And looking remarkably hearty
  For a widow so young in her weeds;
Yet I know she was suffering sorrow
  Too deep for the tongue to express, —
Or why had she chosen to borrow
  So much from the language of dress?

Her shawl was as sable as night;
  And her gloves were as dark as her shawl;
And her jewels — that flashed in the light —
  Were black as a funeral pall;

Her robe had the hue of the rest,
  (How nicely it fitted her shape!)
And the grief that was heaving her breast
  Boiled over in billows of crape!

What tears of vicarious woe,
  That else might have sullied her face,
Were kindly permitted to flow
  In ripples of ebony lace!
While even her fan, in its play,
  Had quite a lugubrious scope,
And seemed to be waving away
  The ghost of the angel of Hope!

Yet rich as the robes of a queen,
  Was the sombre apparel she wore;
I'm certain I never had seen
  Such a sumptuous sorrow before;
And I could n't help thinking the beauty,
  In mourning the loved and the lost,

Was doing her conjugal duty
    Altogether regardless of cost!

One surely would say a devotion
    Performed at so vast an expense,
Betrayed an excess of emotion
    That was really something immense;
And yet as I viewed, at my leisure,
    Those tokens of tender regard,
I thought :.— It is scarce without measure —
    The sorrow that goes by the yard!

Ah! grief is a curious passion;
    And yours — I am sorely afraid —
The very next phase of the fashion
    Will find it beginning to fade;
Though dark are the shadows of grief,
    The morning will follow the night,
Half-tints will betoken relief,
    Till joy shall be symbolled in white!

Ah well!—it were idle to quarrel
   With Fashion, or aught she may do;
And so I conclude with a moral
   And metaphor—warranted new:—
When *measles* come handsomely out,
   The patient is safest, they say;
And the *Sorrow* is mildest, no doubt,
   That works in a similar way!

THE GIFTS OF THE GODS.

THE saying is wise, though it sounds like
    a jest,
That " The gods don't allow us to be in their
    debt,"
For though we may think we are specially blest,
    We are certain to pay for the favors we get!

Are Riches the boon ?   Nay, be not elate ;
    The final account is n't settled as yet ;
Old Care has a mortgage on every estate,
    And that 's what you pay for the wealth that
        you get !

Is Honor the prize ?   It were easy to name
    What sorrows and perils her pathway beset;

Grim Hate and Detraction accompany Fame,
And that's what you pay for the honor you
get!

Is Learning a treasure? How charming the
pair
When Talent and Culture are lovingly met;
But Labor unceasing is grievous to bear,
And that's what you pay for the learning
you get!

Is Genius worth having? There is n't a doubt;
And yet what a price on the blessing is set, —
To suffer more with it than dunces without,
For that's what you pay for the genius you
get!

Is Beauty a blessing? To have it for naught
The gods never grant to their veriest pet;
Pale Envy reminds you the jewel is bought,
And that's what you pay for the beauty you
get!

But Pleasure ?   Alas ! — how prolific of pain !
  Gay Pleasure is followed by gloomy Regret ;
And often Repentance is one of her train,
  And that's what you pay for the pleasure
    you get !

But surely in Friendship we all may secure
  An excellent gift ; never doubt it, — and yet
With much to enjoy there is much to endure,
  And that's what we pay for the friendship
    we get !

But then there is Love ? — Nay, speak not too
    soon ;
  The fondest of hearts may have reason to
    fret ;
For Fear and Bereavement attend on the boon,
  And that's what we pay for the love that we
    get !

And thus it appears — though it sounds like a
    jest —
The gods don't allow us to be in their debt;
And though we may think we are specially blest,
    We are certain to pay for whatever we get!

A CONNUBIAL ECLOGUE.

Arcades ambo,
Et cantare pares et respondere parati.

VIRGIL.

HE.

MUCH lately have I thought, my darling
wife,
Some simple rules might make our wedded life
As pleasant always as a morn in May;
I merely name it, — what does Molly say?

SHE.

Agreed : your plan I heartily approve;
Rules would 'be nice, — but who shall make
them, love?
Nay, do not speak! — let this the bargain be,
One shall be made by you, and one by me,
Till all are done —

HE.

— Your plan is surely fair,
In such a work 't is fitting we should share;
And now — although it matters not a pin —
If you have no objection, I 'll begin.

SHE.

Proceed!   In making laws I 'm little versed;
And as to words, I do not mind the first;
I only claim — and hold the treasure fast —
My sex's sacred privilege, the *last!*

HE.

With all my heart.   Well, dearest, to begin : —
When by our cheerful hearth our friends drop
    in,
And I am talking in my brilliant style
(The rest with rapture listening the while)
About the war, — or anything, in short,
That you 're aware is my especial *forte,* —

Pray don't get up a circle of your own,
And talk of — bonnets, in an undertone !

SHE.

That 's Number One ; I 'll mind it well, if you
Will do as much, my dear, by Number Two :
When we attend a party or a ball,
Don't leave your Molly standing by the wall,
The helpless victim of the dreariest bore
That ever walked upon a parlor-floor,
While you — oblivious of your spouse's doom —
Flirt with the girls, — the gayest in the room !

HE.

When I (although the busiest man alive)
Have snatched an hour to take a pleasant drive,
And say, " Remember, at precisely four
You 'll find the carriage ready at the door,"
Don't keep me waiting half an hour or so,
And then declare, " The clock must be too
    slow ! "

SHE.

When you (such things have happened now
    and then)
Go to the Club with, " I.'ll be back at ten,"
And stay till two o'clock, you need n't say,
" I really was the first to come away;
'T is very strange how swift the time has passed :
I 'm sure, my dear, the clock must be too *fast!*"

HE.

There — that will do; what else remains to say
We may consider at a future day;
I 'm getting sleepy — and — if you have done —

SHE.

Not I! — this making rules is precious fun;
Now here 's another: — When you paint to me
" That charming woman " you are sure to see,
Don't — when you praise the virtues she has
    got —

Name only those you think your wife has not!
And here 's a rule I hope you won't forget,
The most important I have mentioned yet, —
Pray mind it well : — Whenever you incline
To bring your queer companions home to dine,
Suppose, my dear, — Good Gracious ! he 's
   asleep !
Ah ! well, — 't is lucky good advice will keep ;
And he shall have it, or, upon my life,
I 've not the proper spirit of a wife !

THE WIFE'S REVENGE.

FROM THE SPANISH.

I.

"ONCE on a time," there flourished in
Madrid

A painter, clever, and the pet of Fame,

Don José, — but the rest were better hid ;

So please accept the simple Christian name, —

Only, to keep my verse from being prosy,

Pray mind your *Spanish*, and pronounce it,
Hozy!

II.

Don José, — who, it seems, had lately won

Much praise and cash, — to crown a lucky
week,

Resolved for once to have a little fun,
    To ease him of his easel, — so to speak, —
And so, in honor of his limning labors,
He gave a party to his artist-neighbors.

III.

A strange affair ; for not a woman came
    To grace the table ; e'en the painter's spouse,
Donna Casilda, a most worthy dame,
    Was, rather roughly, told to quit the house,
And go and gossip, for the evening, down
Among her cousins in the lower town.

IV.

The lady went ; but presently came back,
    For mirth or mischief, with a jolly cousin,
And sought a closet, where an ample crack
    Revealed the revellers, sitting, by the dozen,
Discussing wine and — Art ? — No, — " women
        folks ! "
    In senseless satire and indecent jokes.

V.

" Women ? " said José, " what do women know
  Of poetry or painting ? " (" Hear him talk !"
Whispered the list'ners.) " When did woman
    show .
A ray of genius in the higher walk
Of either ? No ; to *them* the gods impart
Arts, — quite enough, — but deuce a bit of
    Art ! "

VI.

(" Wretch ! " cried the ladies.) " Yes," said
    José, " take
Away from women love-intrigues and all
The cheap disguises they are wont to make
  To hide their spots, — they 'd sing extremely
    small ! "
(" Fool ! " said his spouse, " we 'll settle, by and
    by,
Who sings the smallest, villain ! — you or I ! ")

VII.

To make the matter worse, the jovial guests
    Were duly mindful not to be exceeded
In coarse allusions and unsavory jests,
    But — following José — talked, of course, as
        he did ;
I 've been, myself, to many a bachelor-party,
And found them, mainly, less refined than hearty.

VIII.

The party over, — full of inward ire,
    Casilda plotted, silently and long,
Some fitting vengeance.   Women seldom tire
    In their resentments, whether right or wrong :
In classic authors we are often warned
There 's   naught   so   savage   as   a   "woman
        scorned."

IX.

Besides, Casilda, be it known, had much
    Of   what   the   French   applaud, — and   not
        amiss, —

As " *savoir-faire* " (I do not know the Dutch);
  The literal Germans call it " *Mutterwiss,* "
The Yankees " *gumption,* " and the Grecians
    " *nous,* " —
A useful thing to have about the house.

X.

At length the lady hit upon a plan
  Worthy of Hermes for its deep disguise;
She got a carpenter, — a trusty man, —
  To make a door, and of a certain size,
With curious carvings and heraldic bands,
And bade him wait her ladyship's commands.

XI.

Then falling sick, — as gentle ladies know
  The ready art, unless romances lie, —
She groaned aloud, and bade Don José go,
  And quickly, too, — or she should surely
    die, —

3 *

And fetch her nurse, — a woman who abode
Some three miles distant by the nearest road.

XII.

With many a frown and many a bitter curse
   He heard the summons. 'T was a pretty
      hour,
He said, — to go a-gadding for a nurse!
   At twelve at night! — and in a drenching
      shower!
He 'd never go, — unless the devil sent, —
And then Don José took his hat and went!

XIII.

A long, long hour he paced the dirty street
   Where dwelt the nurse, but could n't find the
      place;
For he had lost the·number; and his feet,
   Though clad in leather, made a bootless
      chase;

He fain had questioned some one; all in vain,—
The very thieves were fearful of the rain!

XIV.

Returning homeward from his weary tramp,
    He reached his house,— or where his house
        should be;
When, by the glimmer of the entry-lamp,
    Don José saw — and marvelled much to
        see —
An ancient, strange, and most fantastic door,
The like whereof he 'd never seen before!

XV.

" Now, by Our Lady ! — this is mighty queer ! "
    Cried José,— staring at the graven wood, —
" I know my dwelling stands exactly here;
    At least, I 'm certain here is where it stood
Two hours ago, when (here he gave a curse)
Donna Casilda sent me for the nurse.

XVI.

I know the houses upon either side ;

   There stands the dwelling of the undertaker ;

Here my good friend Morena lived and died ;

   And *here 's* the shop of old Trappal, the baker ;

And yet, as sure as iron is n't brass,

'T is not my door, or I 'm a precious ass !

XVII.

" However, I will knock "; and so he did,

   And called, " Casilda! " loud enough to rouse

The very dullest watchman in Madrid ;

   But woke, instead, the porter of the house,

Who rudely asked him, Where he got his beer ?

And bade him, " Go ! — there 's no Casilda

     here ! "

XVIII.

Don José crossed himself in dire dismay,

   Lest he had lost his reason, or his sight ;

At least 't was certain he had lost his way ;
   And, hoping sleep might set the matter right,
He sought and found the dwelling of a friend
Who lived in town — quite at the other end.

XIX.

Next morning José, rising with the sun,
   Returned, once more, to seek the missing
     house ;
And there it stood, as it had always done,
   And there stood also his indignant spouse
With half her city cousins at her back,
Waiting to put poor José on the rack.

XX.

"A charming husband, *you!*" the dame began,
   "To leave your spouse in peril of her life,
For tavern revellers! — You 're a pretty man,
   Thus to desert your lawful, wedded wife,
And spend your nights — O villain! — don't
     explain,
I 'll be revenged if there is law in Spain!"

XXI.

" Nay, Madam, hear me! — just a single
        word — "
And then he told her of his fruitless search
To find the beldam; and of what occurred, —
How his own house had left him in the lurch!
Here such a stream of scorn came pouring in,
Don José's voice was smothered in the din.

XXII.

" Nay," said Casilda, " *that* will never do;
    Your own confession plainly puts you down!
Say you were tipsy, (it were nothing new,)
    And spent the night carousing through the
        town
With other topers; *that* may be received;
But, faith! *your* tale will never be believed!"

XXIII.

Crazed with the clamor of the noisy crew
    All singing chorus to the injured dame,

Say, what the deuce could poor Don José do?—
    He prayed for pardon, and confessed his
        shame;
And gave no dinners, in his future life,
Without remembering to invite his wife!

MIRALDA:

A TALE OF THE ANTILLES.

I.

IN Cuba, when that lovely land
   Saw Tacon reigning in his glory,
How Justice held, at his command,
Her balance with an even hand —
   Learn while you listen to my story.

II.

Miralda — such her maiden name —
   Was poor and fair, and gay and witty,
Yet in Havana not a dame
In satin had a fairer fame,
   Or owned a face one half so pretty.

III.

For years she plied her humble trade,
   (To sell cigars was her vocation,)
And many a gay gallant had paid
More pounds to please the handsome maid
   Than pence to buy his soul's salvation.

IV.

But though the maiden, like the sun,
   Had smiles for every transient rover,
Her smiles were all the bravest won;
Miralda gave her heart to none
   Save Pedro, her affianced lover;

V.

Pedro, a manly youth who bore
   His station well as labor's vassal,
The while he plied a nimble oar
For passengers, from shore to shore,
   Between the Punta and the Castle.

E

VI.

The handsome boatman she had learned
  To love with fondest, truest passion;
For him she saved the gold she earned;
For him Miralda proudly spurned
  The doubtful suit of men of fashion.

VII.

Of these — a giddy, gaudy train,
  Strict devotees of wanton Pleasure —
Gay Count Almonté sought to gain
Miralda's love; but all in vain;
  Her heart was still her Pedro's treasure.

VIII.

At last the Count, in sheer despair
  Of gaining aught by patient suing,
Contrived — the wretch! — a cunning snare,
By wicked force to win and wear
  The prize that spurned his gentler wooing.

IX.

One day a dashing Captain came,
    Before the morning sun had risen,
And, bowing, begged to know her name.
" Miralda."   " Faith ! it is the same.
    Here, men, conduct the girl to prison ! "

X.

" By whose authority ? " she said ;
    " The Governor's ! "   " Nay, then 't is folly
To question more."   She dropped her head,
And followed where the Captain led,
    O'erwhelmed with deepest melancholy.

XI.

The prison seems a league or more
    From poor Miralda's humble shanty ;
Was e'er such treachery before ?
The Count Almonté's at the door,
    To hand her down from the volanté !

XII.

" Ah ! — coward ! " cried the angry maid ;
　" This scurvy trick ! — if Tacon knew it,
Your precious ' Captain,' I 'm afraid,
Would miss, for once, his dress-parade !
　Release me, Count, or you may rue it ! "

XIII.

" Nay," said the Count, " that may not be ;
　I cannot let you go at present ;
I 'll lock you up awhile," said he ;
" If you are lonely, send for me ;
　I 'll try to make your prison pleasant."

XIV.

Poor Pedro ! guess the lad's dismay —
　His stark astonishment at learning
His lady-love had gone away,
(But how or whither none could say,)
　And left no word about returning !

XV.

The man who wrote that "Love is blind"
   Could ne'er have known a genuine lover;
Poor Pedro gave his anxious mind
Miralda's hiding-place to find,
   And found it ere the day was over!

XVI.

Clad in a friar's garb, he hies
   At night to where his love is hidden,
And, favored by his grave disguise,
He learns that she is safe, — and flies,
   As he had entered, unforbidden.

XVII.

What could he do? he pondered long
   On every plausible suggestion;
Alas! the rich may do a wrong,
And buy their quittance with a song,
   If any dare the deed to question!

XVIII.

" Yet *Rumor* whispered long ago,
　　(Although she 's very fond of lying,)
' *Tacon loves justice !* ' — may be so ;
Quien sabe ? — Let his answer show ! —
　　I 'll go and see, — it is but trying ! "

XIX.

And, faith, the boatman kept his word ;
　　To Tacon he the tale related,
Which, when the Governor had heard,
With righteous wrath his breast was stirred.
　　" Swear, boy," he said, " to what you 've
　　　　stated ! "

XX.

He took the oath, and straight began
　　For speedy justice to implore him :
Great Tacon frowned, " Be silent, man ! "
Then called the guard, — away they ran, —
　　And soon the culprit stood before him !

XXI.

Miralda too was standing near,
　To witness to his dark transgression ;
" Know you, my lord, why you are here ? "
" Yes, Excellencia, it is clear
　That I must plead an indiscretion."

XXII.

" The uniform your servants wore
　In this affair, — how came they by it ?
Whose sword was that your Captain bore ?
The crime is grave."　" Nay, I implore
　Your clemency, — I can't deny it."

XXIII.

" This damsel here, — has any stain
　By act of yours been put upon her ? "
" No, Excellencia ; all in vain
Were bribes and threats her will to gain, —
　I here declare it on my honor ! "

XXIV.

"Enough!" the Governor replied,
   And added, in a voice of thunder,
"Go, bring a Priest!"   What *can* betide?
To shrive? to wed? who can decide?
   All stood and mused in silent wonder.

XXV.

The Priest was brought, — a reverend head,
   His hands with holy emblems laden.
"Now, Holy Father, please to wed,
And let the rite be quickly sped,
   Senor Almonté and this maiden!"

XXVI.

Poor Pedro stood aghast!   With fear
   And deep dismay Miralda trembled;
While Count Almonté, thus to hear
The words of doom that smote his ear,
   His sudden horror ill dissembled!

XXVII.

Too late ! for in that presence none
　Had dared a whisper of negation.
The words were said, — the deed was done, —
The Church had joined the two in one
　Ere they had breath for lamentation !

XXVIII.

The Count rode off with drooping head,
　Cursing his fortune and his folly ;
But ere a mile his steed had sped,
A flash ! — and lo ! — the Count is dead ! —
　Slain by a murderous leaden volley !

XXIX.

Soon came the officer who bore
　The warrant of his execution,
With, " Excellencia, all is o'er ;
Senor Almonté is no more ;
　Sooth ! — 't was a fearful retribution ! "

4

XXX.

" Now let the herald," Tacon said,

  " (That none these doings may disparage,)

Proclaim Senor Almonté dead ;

And that Miralda take, instead,

  His lands, now hers by lawful marriage ! "

XXXI.

And so it was the lovers came

  To happiness beyond their dreaming,

And ever after blessed the name

Of him who spared a maiden's shame,

  And spoiled a villain's wicked scheming.

LOVE AND LAW.

A LEGEND OF BOSTON.

I.

JACK NEWMAN was in love; a common
　　case
　With boys just verging upon manhood's
　　prime,
When every damsel with a pretty face
　Seems some bright creature from a purer
　　clime,
Sent by the gods to bless a country town;
A pink-cheeked angel in a muslin gown.

II.

Jack was in love; and also much in doubt,
　(As thoughtful lovers oft have been before,)

If it were better to be in or out, —
   Such pain alloyed his bliss. On reason's
     score,
Perhaps 't is equally a sin to get
Too deep in love, in liquor, or in debt.

III.

The lady of his love, Miss Mary Blank,
   (I call her so to hide her real name,)
Was fair and twenty, and in social rank, —
    That is, in riches, — much above her
     " flame " ;
The daughter of a person who had tin,
Already won ; while Jack had his to win.

IV.

Her father was a lawyer ; rather rusty
   In legal lore, but one who well had striven
In former days to swell his " *res angustæ* "
    To broad possessions ; and, in short, had
     thriven

Bravely in his vocation; though, the fact is,
More by his "practices" ('t was said) than
    practice !

v.

A famous man was Blank for sound advice
    In doubtful cases; for example, where
The point in question is extremely nice,
    And turns upon the section of a hair;
Or where — which seems a very common
    bother —
Justice looks one way, and the Law another.

vi.

Great was his skill to make or mar a plot;
    To prop, at need, a rotten reputation,
Or undermine a good one; he had got
    By heart the subtle science of evasion,
And knew the useful art to pick a flaw
Through which a rascal might escape the law.

VII.

Jack was his pupil; and 't is rather queer
  So shrewd a counsellor did not discover,
With all his cunning both of eye and ear,
  That this same pupil was his daughter's lover;
And — what would much have shocked his
      legal tutor —
Was even now the girl's accepted suitor!

VIII.

Fearing a *non-suit*, if the lawyer knew
  The case too soon, Jack kept it to himself, —
And, stranger still, the lady kept it too;
  For well he knew the father's pride of pelf,
Should e'en a bare suspicion cross his mind,
Would soon abate the action they designed.

IX.

For Jack was impecunious; and Blank
  Had small regard for people who were poor;

Riches to him were beauty, grace, and rank :
   In short, the man was one of many more
Who worship money-bags and those who own
     'em,
And think a handsome sum the *summum bonum.*

X.

I 'm fond of civil words, and do not wish
   To be satirical ; but none despise
The poor so truly as the *nouveaux riche ;*
   And here, no doubt, the real reason lies,
That being over-proud of what they are,
They 're naturally ashamed of what they were.

XI.

Certain to meet the father's cold negation,
   Jack dare not ask him for his daughter's
     hand ;
What should he do ? 'T was surely an occasion
   For all the wit a lover might command ;

At last he chose (it seemed his only hope)
That final card of Cupid, — to elope !

XII.

A pretty plan to please a penny-a-liner ;
    But far less pleasant for the leading factor,
Should the fair maiden chance to be a *minor*,
    (Whom the law reckons an unwilling actor,)
And here Jack found a rather sad obstruction,—
He might be caught and punished for abduction.

XIII.

What could he do ?   Well,—here is what he
      did,
    As a " moot-case " to Lawyer Blank he told
The whole affair, save that the names were hid ;
    I can't help thinking it was rather bold,
But Love is partial to heroic schemes,
And often proves much wiser than he seems.

XIV.

"The thing is safe enough, with proper care,"
　　Observed　the　lawyer,　smiling.　"Here's
　　　your　course : —
Just let the lady manage the affair
　　Throughout ; *Videlicet*, she gets the horse,
And mounts him, unassisted, *first ;* but mind,
The woman sits before, and you, behind !

XV.

"Then who is the abductor ? — Just suppose
　　A court and jury looking at the case ;
What ground of action do the facts disclose ?
　　They find a horse, — two riders, — and a
　　　race, —
And you 'Not Guilty' ; for 't is clearly true
The dashing damsel ran away with you !"

XVI.

* 　 * 　 * 　 * 　 *

4*　　　　　　　　　　　　F

XVII.

These social sins are often rather grave;

  I give such deeds no countenance of mine;

Nor can I say the father e'er forgave;

  But that was surely a propitious " sign,"

On which (in after years) the words I saw

Were, " BLANK AND NEWMAN, COUNSELLORS AT

  LAW!"

SOME PENCIL-PICTURES:

TAKEN AT SARATOGA.

I.

YOUR novel-writers make their ladies tall;
    I mean their heroines; as if, indeed,
It were a fatal failing to be small.
    In this, I own, we are not well agreed, —
I like a little woman, if she 's pretty,
Modest and clever, sensible and witty.

II.

And such is she who sits beside me; fair
    As her deportment; mine is not the pen
To paint the glory of her Saxon hair,
    And eyes of heavenly azure! There are men

Who doat on raven tresses, and are fond
Of dark complexions, — I adore a *blonde!*

.

III.

There sits a woman of another type ;
   Superb in figure and of stately size ;
An Amazonian beauty round and ripe
   As Cytherea, — with delicious eyes
That laugh or languish with a shifting hue
Somewhat between a hazel and a blue.

IV.

Across the room — to please a daintier taste —
   A slender damsel flits with fairy tread ;
A lover's hand might span her little waist,
   If so inclined, — that is, if they were wed.
Some youths admire those fragile forms, I 've
     heard ;
I never saw the *man,* upon my word !

V.

But styles of person, though they please me more,
　(As Nature's work) excite my wonder less
Than all my curious vision may explore
　In moods and manners, equipage and dress ;
The last alone were theme enough, indeed,
For more than I could write, or you would read.

VI.

Swift satirized mankind with little ruth,
　And womankind as well ; but we must own
His words of censure oft are very truth, —
　For instance, where the satirist has shown
How — thankless for the gifts which they have
　　　got —
All strive to show the talents they — have not !

VII.

Thus (it is written) Frederick the Great
　Cared little for the battles he had fought,

But listened eagerly and all-elate

　　To hear a courtier praise the style and thought

That graced his Sonnets; tho' in fact, his verse

　　(I've tried to read it) could n't well be worse!

·   VIII.

The like absurd ambition you may note

　　In fashionable women.　Look you there!

Observe an arm which all (but she) must vote

　　Extremely ugly, — so she keeps it bare

(Lest so much beauty should escape the light)

From wrist to shoulder, morning, noon, and

　　　　night!

IX.

Observe again (the girl who stands alone)

　　How Pride reveals what Prudence would sup-

　　　　press;

A mere anatomy of skin-and-bone, —

　　She wears, of course, a *décolleté* dress!

Those tawny angles seek no friendly screen,
But court the day, and glory to be seen !

X.

O Robert Burns ! if such a thing might be,
   That all by ignorance or folly blind,
For once should " see themselves as others see,"
   (As thou didst pray for hapless human kind,)
What startled crowds would madly rush to hide
The dearest objects of their fondest pride !

ODE TO THE PRINCE OF WALES.

INVITING HIS ROYAL HIGHNESS TO A COUNTRY COTTAGE.

O PRINCE of Wales !
  Unless my judgment fails,
You 've found your recent travel rather dreary ;
I don't expect an answer to the query, —
  But are n't you getting weary ?
Weary of Bells, and Balls, and grand Addresses ?
Weary of Military and their messes ?
Weary of adulation and caresses ?
Weary of shouts from the admiring masses ?
Weary of worship from the upper classes ?
Weary of horses, may'rs, and asses ?

Of course 't was kindly meant, —
But don't you now repent
Your good Mamma's consent
        That you should *be,*
        This side the sea,
The " British *Lion* " which you represent ?
Pray leave your city courtiers and their capers,
And come to us ; we 've no pictorial papers :
And no Reporters to distort your nose ;
Or mark the awkward carriage of your toes ;
Your style of sneezing, and such things as those ;
Or, meaner still, in democratic spite,
Measure your Royal Highness by your height !

        Then come to us !
We 're not the sort of folk to make a fuss,
E'en for the PRESIDENT, — but then, my boy,
We plumply promise you a special joy,
        To Princes rarely known,
(And one you 'll never find about a throne,)

To wit, the bliss of being *let alone!*

No scientific bores from Athenæums ;

No noisy guns, nor tedious *te-deums,*

Shall vex your Royal Highness for a minute ;

A glass of lemonade, with " something in it,"

A fragrant meerschaum, with the morning news,

Or sweet Virginia "fine-cut,"— if you choose,—

These, and what else your Highness may demand

Of simple luxury, shall be at hand,

And at your royal service.   *Come!*

O come where you may gain

(What advertisers oft have sought in vain)

    " The comforts of a home! "

Come, Prince of Wales ! — we greatly need

Your royal presence, Sir, — we do indeed :

For why ? — we have a pretty hamlet here,

But then, you see, 't is equally as clear

(Your   Highness   understands   Shakespearian

      hints)

A *Hamlet* is n't much without a *Prince!*

WHEN I MEAN TO MARRY.

WHEN do I mean to marry? — Well, —
  'T is idle to dispute with fate;
But if you choose to hear me tell,
  Pray listen while I fix the date.

When daughters haste, with eager feet,
  A mother's daily toil to share;
Can make the puddings which they eat,
  And mend the stockings which they wear;

When maidens look upon a man
  As in himself what they would marry,
And not as army-soldiers scan
  A sutler or a commissary;

When gentle ladies, who have got
    The offer of a lover's hand,
Consent to share his earthly lot,
    And do not mean his lot of land;

When young mechanics are allowed
    To find and wed the farmers' girls
Who *don't* expect to be endowed
    With rubies, diamonds, and pearls;

When wives, in short, shall freely give
    Their hearts and hands to aid their spouses,
And live as they were wont to live
    Within their sires' one-story houses;

Then, madam, — if I'm not too old, —
    Rejoiced to quit this lonely life,
I'll brush my beaver; cease to scold;
    And look about me for a wife!

ABOUT HUSBANDS.

"A man is, in general, better pleased when he has a good dinner upon his table, than when his wife speaks Greek." — SAM. JOHNSON.

JOHNSON was right. I don't agree to all.
    The solemn dogmas of the rough old
        stager;
But very much approve what one may call
    The minor morals of the " Ursa Major."

Johnson was right. Although some men adore
    Wisdom in woman, and with learning cram
        her,
There is n't one in ten but thinks far more
    Of his own grub than of his spouse's grammar.

I know it is the greatest shame in life ;
   But who among them (save, perhaps, myself)
Returning hungry home, but asks his wife
   What beef — not books — she has upon the
      shelf ?

Though Greek and Latin be the lady's boast,
   They 're little valued by her loving mate ;
The kind of tongue that husbands relish most
   Is modern, boiled, and served upon a plate.

Or if, as fond ambition may command,
   Some home-made verse the happy matron
      show him,
What mortal spouse but from her dainty hand
   Would sooner see a pudding than a poem ?

Young lady, — deep in love with Tom or
      Harry, —
   'T is sad to tell you such a tale as this ;

But here's the moral of it : Do not marry ;
　　Or, marrying, take your lover as he is, —

A very man, — with something of the brute,
　　(Unless he prove a sentimental noddy,)
With passions strong and appetite to boot, —
　　A thirsty soul within a hungry body.

A very man, — not one of nature's clods, —
　　With human failings, whether saint or sinner ;
Endowed, perhaps, with genius from the gods,
　　But apt to take his temper from his dinner.

THE SUPERFLUOUS MAN.

It is ascertained by inspection of the registers of many countries, that the uniform proportion of male to female births is as 21 to 20 : accordingly, in respect to marriage, every 21st man is naturally superfluous. — TREATISE ON POPULATION.

I LONG have been puzzled to guess,
 And so I have frequently said,
What the reason could really be
 That I never have happened to wed ;
But now it is perfectly clear
 I am under a natural ban ;
The girls are already assigned, —
 And I 'm a superfluous man !

Those clever statistical chaps
 Declare the numerical run

Of women and men in the world,
   Is Twenty to Twenty-and-one ;
And hence in the pairing, you see,
   Since wooing and wedding began,
For every connubial score,
   They 've got a superfluous man !

By twenties and twenties they go,
   And giddily rush to their fate,
For none of the number, of course,
   Can fail of a conjugal mate ;
But while they are yielding in scores
   To Nature's inflexible plan,
There 's never a woman for me, —
   For I 'm a superfluous man !

It is n't that I am a churl,
   To solitude over-inclined ;
It is n't that I am at fault
   In morals or manners or mind ;

Then what is the reason, you ask,
    I 'm still with the bachelor-clan ?
I merely was numbered amiss, —
    And I 'm a superfluous man !

It is n't that I am in want
    Of personal beauty or grace,
For many a man with a wife
    Is uglier far in the face ;
Indeed, among elegant men
    I fancy myself in the van ;
But what is the value of that,
    When I 'm a superfluous man ?

Although I am fond of the girls,
    For aught I could ever discern
The tender emotion I feel
    Is one that they never return ;
'T is idle to quarrel with fate,
    For, struggle as hard as I can,

They 're mated already, you know, —
   And I 'm a superfluous man !

No wonder I grumble at times,
   With women so pretty and plenty,
To know that I never was born
   To figure as one of the Twenty ;
But yet, when the average lot
   With critical vision I scan,
I think it may be for the best
   That I 'm a superfluous man !

TIME AND LOVE.

AN ALLEGORY.

OLD Time and young Love, on a morning in May,
  Chanced to meet by a river in halcyon
    weather,
And, agreeing, for once, ('t is a fable, you 'll
    say,)
  In the same little boat made a voyage to-
    gether.

Strong, steady, and patient, Time pulled at his
    oar,
  And swift o'er the water the voyagers go;

But Love — who was thinking of Pleasure on
    shore —
  Complained that his boatman was wretchedly
    slow.

But Time, the old sailor, expert at his trade,
  And knowing the leagues that remained to
    be done,
Content with the regular speed that he made,
  Tugged away at his oar and kept steadily on.

Love, always impatient of doubt or delay,
  Now sighed for the aid of the favoring gales,
And scolded at Time, in the sauciest way,
  For not having furnished the shallop with
    sails.

But Time, as serene as a calendar saint,
  (Whatever the graybeard was thinking upon,)
All-deaf to the voice of the younker's complaint,
  Tugged away at his oar and kept steadily on.

Love, vexed at the heart, only clamored the
    more,
    And cried, " By the gods ! in what country
        or clime
Was ever a lubber who handled an oar
    In so lazy a fashion as old Father Time ! "

But Time only smiled in a cynical way,
    ('T is often the mode with your elderly Don,)
As one who knows more than he cares to display,
    And still at his oar pulled steadily on.

Grown calmer, at last, the exuberant boy
    Enlivens the minutes with snatches of rhyme ;
The voyage, at length, he begins to enjoy,
    And soon has forgotten the presence of Time !

But Time, the severe, egotistical elf,
    Since the day that his travels he entered upon,
Has ne'er for a moment forgotten himself,
    But tugs at his oar and keeps steadily on.

Awaking, once more, Love sees with a sigh
 That the River of Life will be presently passed,
And now he breaks forth with a piteous cry,
  " O Time, gentle Time ! you are rowing too
   fast ! "

But Time, well knowing that Love will be dead,
 Dead, — dead ! in the boat ! — ere the voyage
  is done,
Only gives him an ominous shake of the head,
 While he tugs at his oar and keeps steadily on !

THE HEART AND THE LIVER.

MUSINGS OF A DYSPEPTIC.

I.

SHE 'S broken-hearted, I have heard,—
 Whate'er may be the reason;
(Such things will happen now and then
 In Love's tempestuous season;)
But still I marvel she should show
 No plainer outward token,
If such a vital inward part
 Were very badly broken!

II.

She 's broken-hearted, I am told,
 And so, of course, believe it;

When truth is fairly certified
    I modestly receive it;
But after such an accident,
    It surely is a blessing;
It does n't in the least impair
    Her brilliant style of dressing!

III.

She 's broken-hearted: who can doubt
    The noisy voice of Rumor?
And yet she seems — for such a wreck —
    In no unhappy humor;
She sleeps (I hear) at proper hours,
    When other folks are dozy;
Her eyes are sparkling as of yore,
    And still her cheeks are rosy!

IV.

She 's broken-hearted, and they say
    She never can recover;

5 *

And then — in not the mildest way —,
   They blame some fickle lover ;
I know she 's dying — by degrees —
   But, sure as I 'm a sinner,
I saw her eat, the other day,
   A most prodigious dinner!

v.

Alas ! that I, in idle rhyme,
   Should e'er profanely question
(As I have done while musing o'er
   My chronic indigestion)
If one should not receive the blow
   With blessings on the Giver,
That only falls upon the heart,
   And kindly spares the LIVER !

THE BEAUTY OF BALLSTON.

(AFTER PRAED.)

IN Ballston — once a famous spot,
　　Ere Saratoga came in fashion —
I had a transient fit of what
　　The poets call the " tender passion " ;
In short, when I was young and gay,
　　And Fancy held the throne of Reason,
I fell in love with Julia May,
　　The reigning beauty of the season.

Her eyes were blue, and such a pair ! —
　　No star in heaven was ever brighter ;
Her skin was most divinely fair ;
　　I never saw a shoulder whiter.

And there was something in her form,
   (An *en-bon-point*, I think they term it,)
That really was enough to warm
   The icy bosom of a hermit !

In sooth, she was a witching girl,
   And even women called her pretty,
Who saw her in the waltz's whirl,
   Beneath the glare of spermaceti ;
Or if they carped — as Candor must
   When wounded pride and envy rankle —
'T was only that so full a bust
   Should heave above so trim an ankle !

One eve, remote from festive mirth,
   We talked of Nature and her treasures ;
I said : — " Of all the joys of earth,
   Pray name the sweetest of her pleasures."
She gazed with rapture at the moon
   That struggled through the spreading
     beeches, —

And answered thus : — " A grove — at noon —
  A friend — and lots of cream and peaches ! "

I spoke of trees, — the stately oak
  That stands the forest's royal leader ;
The whispering pine ; and then I spoke
  Of Lebanon's imperial cedar ;
The maple of our colder clime ;
  The elm with branches intermeeting, —
She thought the palm must be sublime,
  And — dates were very luscious eating !

I talked about the sea and sky,
  And spoke, with something like emotion,
Of countless pearly gems that lie
  Ungathered by the sounding ocean.
She smiled, and said, (was it in jest ?)
  Of all the shells that Nature boasted
She thought that oysters were the best,
  " And, dearest, don't you love 'em roasted ! "

I talked of books and classic lore ;
    I spoke of Cooper's latest fiction,
Recited melodies from Moore,
    And lauded Irvings's charming diction ; —
She sat entranced ; then raised her head,
    And with a smile that seemed of heaven,
" We must return," the siren said,
    " Or we shall lose the lunch at 'leven ! "

I can't describe the dreadful shock,
    The mingled sense of love and pity,
With which, next day, at ten o'clock,
    I started for Manhattan city ;
'T was years ago — that sad " Good bye,"
    Yet o'er the scene fond memory lingers ;
I see the crystals in her eye,
    And berry-stains upon her fingers !

Ah me ! of so much loveliness
    It had been sweet to be the winner ;

I know she loved me only less —

    The merest fraction — than her dinner;

'T was hard to lose so fair a prize,

    But then (I thought) 't were vastly harder

To have before my jealous eyes

    A constant rival in my larder!

TOUJOURS LES FEMMES.

I THINK it was a Persian king
   Who used to say, that evermore
In human life each evil thing
   Comes of the sex that men adore ;
That naught, in brief, had e'er befell
   To harm or grieve our hapless race,
But, if you probe the matter well,
   You 'll find a woman in the case !

And then the curious tale is told
   How, when upon a certain night
A climbing youngster lost his hold,
   And falling from a ladder's height,

Was found, alas! next morning dead,
  His Majesty, with solemn face,
As was his wont, demurely said,
  "Pray, who's the woman in the case?"

And how a lady of his court,
  Who deemed the royal whim absurd,
Rebuked him, while she made report
  Of the mischance that late occurred;
Whereat the king replied in glee,
  "I've heard the story, please your Grace,
And all the witnesses agree
  There was a woman in the case!"

" The truth, your Ladyship, is this,
  (Nor is it marvellous at all)
The chap was climbing for a kiss,
  And got, instead, a fatal fall.
Whene'er a man — as I have said —
  Falls from a ladder. or from grace,

Or breaks his faith, or breaks his head,
   There is a woman in the case!"

For such a churlish, carping creed
   As that his Majesty professed,
I hold him of unkingly breed, —
   Unless, in sooth, he spoke in jest.
To me, few things have come to pass
   Of good event, but I can trace, —
Thanks to the matron or the lass, —
   Somewhere, a woman in the case.

Yet once, while gayly strolling where
   A vast Museum still displays
It's varied wealth of strange and rare,
   To charm, or to repel, the gaze, —
I — to a lady (who denied
   The creed by laughing in my face) —
Took up, for once, the Persian's side
   About a woman in the case.

Discoursing thus, we came upon

    A grim Egyptian mummy — dead ›

Some centuries since. " 'T is Pharaoh's son —

    Perhaps — who knows? " — the lady said.

No ! — on the black sarcophagus

    A female name I stooped to trace ;

Toujours les femmes! — 'T is ever thus —

    There was a woman in the *case!*

THE STAMMERING WIFE.

I.

WHEN, deeply in love with Miss Emily
   Pryne,
I vowed, if the maiden would only be mine,
 I would always endeavor to please her, —
She blushed her consent, tho' the stuttering
   lass
Said never a word, except "You 're an ass —
 An ass — an ass-idubus teaser ! "

II.

But when we were married I found to my ruth
The stammering lady had spoken the truth,
 For often, in obvious dudgeon,

She 'd say, — if I ventured to give her a jog
In the way of reproof, — " You 're a dog —
    you 're a dog —
  A dog — a dog-matic curmudgeon ! "

III.

And once when I said, " We can hardly afford
This extravagant style, with our moderate
    hoard,
  And hinted we ought to be wiser,
She looked, I assure you, exceedingly blue,
And fretfully cried, " You 're a Jew — you 're
    a Jew —
  A very ju-dicious adviser ! "

IV.

Again, when it happened that, wishing to shirk
Some rather unpleasant and arduous work,
  I begged her to go to a neighbor,
She wanted to know why I made such a fuss,

And · saucily said, "You 're a cus — cus —
   cus —

You were always ac-cus-tomed to labor!"

v.

Out of temper at last with the insolent dame,
And feeling that Madam was greatly to blame
   To scold me instead of caressing,
I mimicked her speech — like a churl as I am —
And angrily said, "You 're a dam — dam —
   dam —

A dam-age instead of a blessing!"

NIL ADMIRARI.

I.

WHEN Horace in Vendusian groves
 Was scribbling wit or sipping "Massic,"
Or singing those delicious loves
 Which after ages reckon classic,
He wrote one day — 't was no vagary —
These famous words : — *Nil admirari!*

II.

" Wonder at nothing ! " — said the bard ;
 A kingdom's fall, a nation's rising,
A lucky or a losing card,
 Are really not at all surprising,
However men or manners vary,
Keep cool and calm ; *Nil admirari!*

III.

If kindness meet a cold return ;
　　If friendship prove a dear delusion ;
If love, neglected, cease to burn,
　　Or die untimely of profusion, —
Such lessons well may make us wary,
But need n't shock ; *Nil admirari!*

IV.

Does disappointment follow gain ?
　　Or wealth elude the keen pursuer ?
Does pleasure end in poignant pain ?.
　　Does fame disgust the lucky wooer,
Or haply prove perversely chary ?
'T was ever thus ; *Nil admirari!*

V.

Does January wed with May,
　　Or ugliness consort with beauty ?
Does Piety forget to pray ?
　　And, heedless of connubial duty,

Leave faithful Ann for wanton Mary?
'T is the old tale; *Nil admirari!*

VI.

Ah! when the happy day we reach
　When promisers are ne'er deceivers;
When parsons practise what they preach,
　And seeming saints are all believers,
Then the old maxim you may vary,
And say no more, *Nil admirari!*

ADVICE TO A YOUNG FRIEND,

WHO THINKS HE SHOULD LIKE TO BE A LAWYER.

NO, no, my boy! let others sweat
　　And wrangle in the courts;
Their *Pleas* are most unpleasing things;
　　You cannot trust *Reports!*

Although the law of literature
　　May your attention draw,
I 'm very sure you would n't like
　　The Literature of Law!

Justinian's Novels don't compare
　　With those of Walter Scott;
They 've very little sentiment,
　　And deuce a bit of plot!

When *Coke on Littleton* came down,
   He served him right; but who
Would say it were a civil thing
   To set them both on you?

In *Blackstone* there is much, I own,
   Well worthy of regard;
But then, my boy, like other stones,
   You 'll find him precious hard!

Sir William Jones is very well,
   As every scholar knows;
But read, my lad, his poetry,
   And never mind his prose.

Though *Angell* tempt you, heed him not;
   For Satan, to his shame,
Full oft, to further wicked ends,
   Employs a seraph's name!

Though *Aiken* may be very wise,
    Pray what is that to you?
His reader will be apt to find　.
    That he is achin' too!

There 's *Story* now, the lawyers say,
    Is very fine indeed;
I only know he 's not the kind
    Young fellows like to read!

And as for *Cruise*, though much admired,
    You 'd better let him be,
And use, instead, the milder sort
    That people take at sea!

No, no, my boy! let others sweat
    And wrangle in the courts;
There 's nothing pleasing in a *Plea;*
    You cannot trust *Reports!*

Although the law of literature
    May your attention draw,
I 'm very sure you would n't like
    The Literature of Law !

THE GAME OF LIFE.

A HOMILY.

THERE's a game much in fashion,—I
    think it's called *Euchre;*
(Though I never have played it, for pleasure
    or lucre,)
In which, when the cards are in certain condi-
    tions,
The players appear to have changed their posi-
    tions,
And one of them cries, in a confident tone,
"I think I may venture to *go it alone!*"

While watching the game, 't is a whim of the
    bard's
A moral to draw from that skirmish of cards,

And to fancy he finds in the trivial strife
Some excellent hints for the battle of Life;
Where — whether the prize be a ribbon or
    throne —
The winner is he who can go it alone!

When great Galileo proclaimed that the world
In a regular orbit was ceaselessly whirled,
And got — not a convert — for all of his pains,
But only derision and prison and chains,
" It moves, *for all that!* " was his answering
    tone,
For he knew, like the Earth, he could go it
    alone!

When Kepler, with intellect piercing afar,
Discovered the laws of each planet and star,
And doctors, who ought to have lauded his
    name,
Derided his learning, and blackened his fame,

"I can *wait!*" he replied, " till the truth you
      shall own ";
For he felt in his heart he could go it alone!

Alas! for the player who idly depends,
In the struggle of life, upon kindred or friends;
Whatever the value of blessings like these,
They can never atone for inglorious ease,
Nor comfort the coward who finds, with a
      groan,
That his crutches have left him to go it alone!

There 's something, no doubt, in the hand you
      may hold,
Health, family, culture, wit, beauty, and gold
The fortunate owner may fairly regard
As, each in its way, a most excellent card;
Yet the game may be lost, with all these for
      your own,
Unless you 've the courage to " go it alone! "

In battle or business, whatever the game,
In law or in love, it is ever the same;
In the struggle for power, or the scramble for
      pelf,
Let this be your motto, — *Rely on yourself!*
For, whether the prize be a ribbon or throne,
The victor is he who can go it alone!

THE EDITOR'S CRIME.

WITH a gloomy air,
    And a dreamy stare,
An Editor sits in his sanctum-chair,
Musing like one in trouble or doubt;
And what do you think he is thinking about?

    "I'm sorely afraid
    This wearisome trade
Will waste me away to the veriest shade;
And force me, perhaps,—but that cannot be —
A *murder*'s a horrible crime!" said he.

    "I never shirk
    Editorial work,
Nor mind the libel that in it may lurk;

Miscellaneous matter is easy to choose ;
But the News ! — the *News !* — they *will* have
>> News !

>> A leader to write
>> Or a tale to indite,
Is easy as lying — that is n't the " bite " ;
All wholesome reading the public refuse ;
'T is " News ! " — " *News !* " — " NEWS ! " —
>> they *will* have News !

>> That 's not the worst,
>> My paper is curs'd,
Unless it is crammed, till it 's ready to burst,
With doings at which humanity quails, —
Rapes, Riots and Murders, with all the details !

>> A bloodless row,
>> Or a five-legged cow,
Is quite too tame for an item now ;

" News," — " *News*," — " NEWS ! " — is still the
  song,
And then they *will* have it so horribly strong !

  'T was but t' other day
  I heard a man say,
He wa'n't to be done in so shabby a way, —
For, of all the crimes my paper could boast,
The worst, for a month, was a " MURDER ! —
  almost."

  Ah ! *malheureux !*
  'T is true ! — 't is true !
But what the deuce can an Editor do ?
If crimes *won't* happen, they don't suppose
I 'm going to make 'em ? — (Ha ! ha ! — who
  knows ?)

  I will — I won't —
  I dare — I don't ! —

I tremble to think I am thinking upon 't!
The blackest of frowns is clouding his brow, —
O, what is the Editor muttering now?

On the following day,
In a flaming way,
The *Pepperville Post* was " shocked to say,   .
Our slumbering city was roused last night
By a startling sound, and a horrible sight!

" DIABOLICAL CRIME!
Last night, — sometime, —
Not far from the stroke of the midnight chime,
By some person unknown, with a pistol or gun,
A most unnatural MURDER WAS DONE

" On Jonathan Brown! —
While walking down
The principal street of our beautiful town, —
A citizen held in the highest regard;
And the Mayor should offer a handsome reward

" For the infamous wretch,
That the rascal may stretch
The best bit of rope in the hands of Jack Ketch!
Post scriptum.   A chap has been lurking about
Whom nobody knows, — the assassin, no doubt.

" STILL LATER !   'T is said
That the murderous lead
Had a conical shape, and went quite through the
head :
Of our wide-awake journal we don't wish
to boast,
But no Pepperville print has the news, but the
POST ! "

I grieve to tell
Suspicion fell
On the man who had told the story so well !
Namely, the Editor ! — none but he
Knew aught of the case, — who else could it be ?

On looking around,
A bullet was found
(Of a conical shape) not far from the ground
Whereon it was known the murder was done, —
A bullet that fitted the Editor's gun!

'T is sad to relate
How the merciless State
Doomed him to suffer a murderer's fate;
And how on the gallows the wicked Editor
Died, — lamented by many a creditor!

But I 'm glad to say
It was told, that day,
Such things are out of the usual way,
And, to the honor of all the *corps*,
Never was Editor hanged before!

FIRST MORAL.

Don't edit a journal!
(That is, a diurnal,)

The labors and dangers are really infernal;

And will drive you, at last, to some folly or

other;

Perhaps to the fate of your Pepperville brother!

SECOND MORAL.

If you choose to regard

Such advice as too hard,

And *will* edit a Daily, in spite of the bard,

Go to *Babylon*,— where, in the dullest of times,

You won't have occasion to do your own

" Crimes! "

THIRD MORAL.

If you *must* have a bite

At eleven at night,

Don't eat lobster-salad, but take something light;

Or, — *crede experto*, — you 'd better beware

Of taking a nap in your sanctum chair!

PADDY'S ODE TO THE PRINCE.

O MIGHTY Prince!
It's no offince,
  Your worship, that I mane ye,
While I confiss
'T was ra-al bliss,
  A moment to have sanc ye!

That you should see
The likes o' me,
  The while I stud adjacent,
I don't suppose,
Although me clo'es
  Was mighty clane and dacent.

Av coorse, ye know
'T was long ago,
   I looked at Jukes and *such* men,
And longer since,
An *English* Prince
   Begotten by a Dutchman!

But by me troth,
And Bible-oath!
   Wid all me Irish shyness,
I 've passed the word
Wid many a lord,
   Much taller than your Highness!

Ah! well, — bedad,
No doubt ye had,
   In token of allagiance,
As good a cup
As ye could sup
   Among thim black Canajans;

But wha' d' ye think
Of Christian dhrink,
  Now tell me *that*, me tulip!
When through a sthraw
Your Highness saw,* .
  The flavor of a *julep?*

Thim haythen chaps,
The nayger *Japs,*
  Wid all their curst expinses,
Just tuk their fill,
And left a bill
  At which the paple winces;

But thin, no doubt,
Ye 'll ride about
  Wid Boole and all the Aldermen;

* The faculty of seeing a flavor is, of course, peculiarly
Hibernian.

They 've little sinse,
But, for expinse,
   There 's not a sèt of boulder men !

FERNANDY WUD
Has dacent blood,
   And illigant morality ;
And ye may swear
Our mighty Mayor
   Will show his horsepitality !

The soldiers all
Are at his call,
   Wid Captains to parade 'em ;
And at the laste,
Ye 'll get a taste
   Of dimmecratic fraydem.

But plase to note,
Ye 're not to *vote*, —
   A privilege, by Jabers !

Ye could n't hope,
Were ye the Pope,
   Until ye 've got the papers!

Well, mighty Prince,
Accept these hints;
   Most frayly I indite 'em;
'T is luck, indade,
If ye can rade
   As aisy as I write 'em!

And when the throne
Is all ye'r own
   At which ye 're daily steerin',
Remimber what
Some kings forgot, —
   Remimber poor ould Erin.

A CASE OF CONSCIENCE.

TWO College Professors, — I won't give
their names, —
(Call one of them *Jacob*, the other one, *James*,)
Two College Professors, who ne'er in their lives
Had wandered before from the care of their
wives, —
One day in vacation, when lectures were
through,
And teachers and students had nothing to do,
Took it into their noddles to go to the Races,
To look at the nags, and examine their paces,
And find out the meaning of "bolting," and
"baiting,"
And the (clearly preposterous) practice of
"waiting,"

And " laying long odds," and the other queer
    capers
Which cram the reports that appear in the
    papers ;
And whether a " stake " is the same as a post ?
And how far a " heat " may resemble a roast ?
And whether a " hedge " in the language of
    sport
Is much like the plain agricultural sort ?
And if " making a book " is a thing which re-
    quires
A practical printer ? — and who are the buy-
    ers ? —
Such matters as these — very proper to
    know —
And no thought of betting — induced them to
    go
To the Annual Races, which then were in force,
(Horse-racing, in fact, is a matter of *course*,
Apart from the pun ;) in a neighboring town ;
And so, as I said, the Professors went down.

The day was the finest that ever was known ;
The atmosphere just of that temperate tone
Which pleases the Spirit of (man and) the
        Times,
But impossible, quite, to describe in my rhymes.
The track has been put in a capital plight
By a smart dash of rain on the previous night,
And all things " went off" — save some of the
        horses —
As lively as crickets or Kansas divorces !

Arrived at the ground, it is easy to guess
Our worthy Professors' dismay and distress
At all the queer things which expanded their
        eyes
(Not to mention their ears) to a wonderful
        size !
How they stared at the men who were playing
        at poker,
And scolded the chap with the " sly little
        joker " ;

And the boy who had " something uncommonly
    nice,"
Which he offered to sell at a very high price, —
A volume that did n't seem over-refined,
And clearly was *not* of the Sunday-school kind.
All this, and much more, — but your patience
    will fail,
Unless I desist, and go on with my tale.

Our worthy Professors no sooner had found
Their (ten-shilling) seats in the circular ground,
And looked at the horses, — when, presently,
    came
A wish to know what was the *Favorite's* name;
And how stood the *betting*, — quite plainly re-
    vealing
The old irrepressible horse-race-y feeling
Which is born in the bone, and is apt to come
    out
When thorough-bred coursers are snorting
    about !

The Professors, in fact, — I am grieved to re-
    port, —
At the very first match entered into the sport,
And bet (with each other) their money away —
Just *Fifty* a-piece — on the *Brown* and the
    Bay;
And shouted as loud as they ever could bellow,
" Hurrah for the filly ! " and " Go it, old fel-
    low ! "
And, " Stick to your business ! " and " Rattle
    your pegs ! " —
Like a jolly old brace of professional " Legs ! "

The race being over, quoth *Jacob,* " I see
My wager is forfeit ; to *that* I agree.
The *Fifty* is yours, by the technical rules
Observed, I am told, by these horse-racing fools;
But then, as a *Christian,* — I 'm sorry to say
    it, —
My Conscience, you know, won't allow me to
    pay it ! "

"No matter,"—quoth *James*,—"I can hardly
     refuse

To accord with your sound theological views:

A tardy repentance is better than none;

I must tell you, however, 't was *your* horse that
     won!

But of course you won't think of demanding
     the pelf,

For *I* have a conscience as well as yourself!"

THE MONARCH AND THE MARQUIS.

AN ORIENTAL LEGEND.

I.

IT was a merry monarch
　　Who ruled a distant land,
And ever, for his pastime,
　　Some new device he planned,
And once, to all his servants,
　　He gave this queer command : —

II.

Quoth he, "To every stranger
　　Who comes unto my court,
Let a fried fish be given,
　　And of the finest sort,

Then mark the man's behavior,
  And bring me due report.

III.

If, when the man has eaten
  The fish unto the bone,
The glutton turns it over —
  Then, by my royal throne,
For this, his misdemeanor,
  The gallows shall atone!"

IV.

Now when this regal mandate,
  According to report,
Had slain a score of strangers,
  To serve the monarch's sport,
It chanced a gay young Marquis
  Came to the royal court.

V.

His majesty received him
  As suited with his state,

But when he sat at dinner,
  The fish was on the plate;
Alas! he turns it over,
  Unconscious of his fate.

VI.

Then, to his dire amazement,
  Three guardsmen, standing nigh,
Conveyed him straight to prison,
  And plainly told him why, —
And how, in retribution,
  That he was doomed to die!

VII.

The Marquis, filled with sorrow,
  Implored the monarch's ruth,
Whereat the King relented,
  (A gracious deed, in sooth!)
And granted these conditions,
  In pity of his youth: —

VIII.

That for three days the culprit
    Should have the King's reprieve;
Also, to name three wishes
    The prisoner had leave —
One each succeeding morning —
    The which he should receive.

IX.

"Thanks!" said the grateful Marquis,
    "His Majesty is kind;
And, first, to wed his daughter
    Is what I have in mind;
Go, bid him fetch a parson
    The holy tie to bind."

X.

Now when the merry monarch
    This bold demand had heard,

With grief and indignation
  His royal breast was stirred;
But he had pledged his honor,
  And so he kept his word.

XI.

Now if the first petition
  He reckoned rather bold,
What was the King's amazement
  To hear the second told, —
To wit, the monarch's treasure
  Of silver and of gold!

XII.

To beg the culprit's mercy
  This mighty King was fain;
But pleading and remonstrance ·
  Were uttered all in vain;
And so he gave the treasure
  It cost him years to gain.

XIII.

Sure ne'er was mortal monarch
    In such dismay as he !
He woke next morning early
    And went, himself, to see
What, in the name of wonder,
    The third demand would be !

XIV.

" I ask," replied the Marquis,
    (" My third and final wish,)
That you should call the servants
    Who served the fatal dish,
And have the eyes extinguished
    That saw me turn the fish."

XV.

" Good !" said the monarch gayly,
    With obvious delight,

" What you demand, Sir Marquis,
   Is reasonable — quite ;
That they should pay this forfeit
   Is nothing more than right.

XVI.

" How was it — Mr. Chamberlain ? "
   But he at once denied
That he had seen the culprit
   Turn up the other side ;
" It must have been the Steward,"
   The Chamberlain replied.

XVII.

" Indeed ! " exclaimed the Steward,
   " It surely was n't I ! —
It must have been the Butler " —
   Who quickly made reply,
" It must have been the guardsmen,
   Unless the fellows lie ! "

XVIII.

But they, in turn, protested,
   With plausible surprise,
(And dreadful imprecations,
   If they were telling lies!)
That nothing of the matter
   Had come before their eyes!

XIX.

" Good Father," — said the Princess,
   " I pray you ponder this : —
(And here she gave the monarch
   A reverential kiss)
My husband must be guiltless,
   If none saw aught amiss ! "

XX.

The monarch frowned a little,
   And gravely shook his head ;

" Your Marquis should be punished ;
　　Well, let him live," he said,
" For though he cheats the gallows,
　　The man, at least, is wed ! "

THE FOUR MISFORTUNES.

A HEBREW TALE.

I.

A PIOUS Rabbi, forced by heathen hate
　　To quit the boundaries of his native
　　　　land,
Wandered abroad, submissive to his fate,
　　Through pathless woods and wastes of burn-
　　　　ing sand.

II.

A patient ass, to bear him in his flight,
　　A dog, to guard him from the robber's stealth,
A lamp, by which to read the law at night,—
　　Was all the pilgrim's store of worldly wealth.

III.

At set of sun he reached a little town,
 And asked for shelter and a crumb of food;
But every face repelled him with a frown,
 And so he sought a lodging in the wood.

IV.

" 'T is very hard," the weary traveller said,
 " And most inhospitable, I protest,
To send me fasting to this forest bed;
 But God is good, and means it for the best!"

V.

He lit his lamp to read the sacred law,
 Before he spread his mantle for the night;
But the wind rising with a sudden flaw,
 He read no more,—the gust put out the light.

VI.

" 'T is strange," he said, " 't is very strange, indeed,
 That ere I lay me down to take my rest,

A chapter of the law I may not read, —
    But God is good, and all is for the best."

VII.

With these consoling words the Rabbi tries
    To sleep, — his head reposing on a log, —
But, ere he fairly shut his drowsy eyes,
    A wolf came up and killed his faithful dog.

VIII.

" What new calamity is this ? " he cried ;
    " My honest dog — a friend who stood the test
When others failed — lies murdered at my side !
    Well, — God is good and means it for the
        best."

IX.

Scarce had the Rabbi spoken, when, alas ! —
    As if, at once, to crown his wretched lot,
A hungry lion pounced upon the ass,
    And killed the faithful donkey on the spot.

X.

" Alas ! — alas ! "— the weeping Rabbi said,
  " Misfortune haunts me like a hateful guest ;
My dog is gone, and now my ass is dead, —
  Well, — God is good, and all is for the best ! "

XI.

At dawn of day, imploring heavenly grace,
  Once more he sought the town ; but all in
    vain ;
A band of robbers had despoiled the place,
  And all the churlish citizens were slain !

XII.

" Now God be praised ! " the grateful Rabbi
    cried,
  " If I had tarried in the town to rest,
I too, with these poor villagers, had died, —
  Sure, God is good, and all is for the best !

XIII.

" Had not the saucy wind put out my lamp,
   By which the sacred law I would have read,
The light had shown the robbers to my camp,
   And here the villains would have left me
      dead !

XIV.

" Had not my faithful animals been slain,
   Their noise, no doubt, had drawn the robbers
      near,
And so their master, it is very plain,
   Instead of them, had fallen murdered here !

XV.

" Full well I see that this hath happened so
   To put my faith and patience to the test ;
Thanks to His name ! for now I surely know
   That God is good, and all is for the best ! "

OTHELLO, THE MOOR.

A TRAVESTY.

ROMANCES of late are so wretchedly poor,
    Here goes for the old one: — Othello
        the Moor;
A warrior of note, and by no means a boor,
    Though the skin on his face
    Was black as the ace
Of spades; or (a simile nearer the case)
Say, black as the Deuce; or black as a brace
Of very black cats in a very dark place!
    That's the German idea;
    But how he *could* be a
Regular negro don't seem very clear;

For Horace, you know,

A great while ago,

Put a sentiment forth which we all must agree

to :

" *Hic niger est; hunc tu, Romane, caveto !*"

(A nigger 's a rascal that one ought to see to.)

I rather, in sooth,

Think it nearer the truth

To take the opinion of young Mr. Booth,

Who makes *his* Othello

A grim-looking fellow

Of a color compounded of lamp-black and yel-

low.

Now Captain Othello, a true son of Mars,

The foe being vanquished, returned from the

wars,

All covered with ribbons, and garters, and

stars,

Not to mention a score of magnificent scars ;

And calling, one day,

In a neighborly way,

On Signor Brabantio — one of the men

Who figured in Venice as Senator then —

Was invited to tell

Of all that befell

Himself and his friends while campaigning so

· well,

From the time of his boyhood till now he was

grown

The greatest of Captains that Venice had known.

As a neighbor should do,

He ran it quite through,

(I would n't be bail it was all of it true)

Recounting, with ardor, such trophies and glo-

ries,

Among Ottoman rebels and Cyprian tories,

Not omitting a parcel of cock-and-bull stories, —

That he quite won the heart of the Senator's

daughter,

Who, like most of the sex, had a passion for
      slaughter ;
    And was wondrously bold
    In battles — as told
By brilliant romancers, who picture in gold
What, in its own hue, you 'd be shocked to be-
      hold.

Now Captain Othello, who never had known a
Young lady so lovely as " Fair Desdemona,"
Not even his patroness, Madam Bellona, —
    Was delighted, one day,
    At hearing her say,
Of all men in the world he 'd the charmingest
    way
Of talking to women ; and if any one *should*,
(Tho' she did n't imagine that any one would, —
For where, to be sure, was another who *could?*)
But, *if* — and *suppose* — a lover came to her,
And told her *his* story, 'twould certainly woo
      her.

With so lucid a hint,

The dickens were in 't,

If he could n't have read her as easy as print;

And thus came of course, — but as to the rest, —

The billing and cooing I leave to be guessed, —

And how when their passion was fairly confessed,

They sent for a parson to render them " blest," —

Although it was done, I am sorry to say,

In what Mrs. P. — had it happened to-day —

Would be likely to call a *clam-destiny* way !

I cannot recount

One half the amount

Of curses that burst from his cardiac fount

When Signor Brabantio learned that the Moor

Had married his daughter ; " How *dared* he to
woo her ?

The sooty-skinned knave, — thus to blight and
undo her !

With what villanous potions the scoundrelly
sinner

Must have poisoned her senses in order to win

her! "

And more of the same, —

But my language is lame,

E'en a fishwoman's tongue were decidedly tame

A tithe of the epithets even to name,

Compounded of scorn and derision and hate,

Which Signor Brabantio poured on the pate

Of the beautiful girl's nigritudinous mate!

I cannot delay

To speak of the way

The matter was settled ; suffice it to say

'T was exactly the same as you see in a play,

Where the lady persuades her affectionate sire,

That the fault was her own, — which softens his

ire,

And, though for a season extremely annoyed,

At last he approves — what he cannot avoid!

Philosophers tell us

A mind like Othello's, —

Spurned all explanation the dame could afford,
And still kept repeating the odious word,
So false, and so foul to a virtuous ear,
That I could n't be tempted to mention it
        here.
        'T is sadder to tell
        Of the crime that befel,
When, moved, it would seem, by the demons
        of hell,
        He seized a knife,
        And, kissing his wife,
Extinguished the light of her innocent life ;
And how, also, before the poor body was cool,
He found he had acted as villany's tool,
And died exclaiming, " O fool ! *fool !* FOOL ! "

MORAL.

Young ladies ! — beware of hasty connections ,
And don't marry suitors with swarthy complex-
        ions ;

For though they may chance to be capital fel-
         lows,
Depend upon it, they 're apt to be jealous!

Young gentlemen! pray recollect, if you can,
To give a wide berth to a meddlesome man ;
And horsewhip the knave who would poison
         your life
By breeding distrust between you and your wife!

VENUS AND VULCAN:

OR, THE MYSTERY EXPLAINED.

WHEN the peerless Aphrodite
    First appeared among her kin,
What a flutter of excitement
    All the goddesses were in!

How the gods, in deep amazement,
    Bowed before the Queen of Beauty,
And in loyal adoration
    Proffered each his humble duty!

Phœbus, first, to greet her coming,
    Met her with a grand oration;
Mars, who ne'er before had trembled,
    Showed the plainest trepidation!

Hermes fairly lost his cunning,
  Gazing at the new Elysian ;
Plutus quite forgot his money
  In the rapture of his vision !

Even Jove was deeply smitten,
  (So the Grecian poets tell us,)
And, as might have been expected,
  Juno was extremely jealous !

Staid Minerva thought her silly ;
  Chaste Diana called her vain ;
But not one of all the ladies
  Dared to say that she was " plain " !

Surely such a throng of lovers
  Never mortal yet could boast ;
Everywhere throughout Olympus
  " Charming Venus ! " was the toast !

Even Vulcan, lame and ugly,
 Paid the dame his awkward court;
But the goddess, in derision,
 Turned his passion into sport;

Laughed aloud at all his pleading;
 Bade him wash his visage sooty,
And go wooing with the Harpies,
 What had *he* to do with Beauty?

Well — how fared it with the goddess?
 Sure, the haughty queen of love,
Choosing one to suit her fancy,
 Married Phœbus, Mars or Jove?

No! — at last — as often happens
 To coquettes of lower station —
Venus found herself neglected,
 With a damaged reputation;

And esteeming any husband
　　More desirable than none,
She was glad to marry Vulcan
　　As the best that could be done !

L'ENVOI.

Hence you learn the real reason,
　　Which your wonder oft arouses,
Why so many handsome women
　　Have such very ugly spouses !

JUPITER AND DANAĖ:

OR, HOW TO WIN A WOMAN.

IMPERIAL Jove, who, with wonderful art,
    Was one of those suitors that always pre-
        vail,
Once made an assault on so flinty a heart,
    That he feared for a while he was destined
        to fail.

A beautiful maiden, Miss Danaë by name,
    The Olympian lover endeavored to win;
But she peeped from the casement whenever
        he came,
Exclaiming, "You're handsome, but cannot
        come in!"

With sweet adulation he tickled her ear; .
 But still at her window she quietly sat,
And said, though his speeches were pleasant to
  hear,
 She 'd always been used to such homage as
  that !

Then he spoke, in a fervid and rapturous strain,
 Of a bosom consuming with burning desire;
But his eloquent pleading was wholly in vain, —
 She thought it imprudent to meddle with fire !

Then he begged her in mercy to pity his case,
 And spoke of his dreadfully painful condition ;
But the lady replied, with a sorrowful face,
 She was only a maiden, and not a physi-
  cian !

In vain with these cunning conventional snares,
 To win her the gallant Lothario strove ;

In spite of his smiles, and his tears, and his
    . prayers,
  She could n't, she would n't, be courted by
    Jove !

At last he contrived, — so the story is told, —
  By some means or other, one evening, to pour
Plump into her apron a shower of gold,
  Which opened her heart — and unbolted her
    door !

L'ENVOI.

Hence suitors may learn that in matters of love
  'T is idle in manners or merit to trust ;
The only sure way is to imitate Jove, —
  Just open your purse, and come down with
    the dust !

THE PARROT OF NEVERS.

I.

ONCE on a time there flourished in Nevers,
   Within a nunnery of godly note,
A famous parrot, so exceeding fair
   In the deep lustre of his emerald coat,
They called him Ver-Vert — syllables that mean
In English much the same as Double Green.

II.

In youth transplanted from an Indian strand,
   For his soul's health with Christian folks to
      dwell,
His morals yet were pure, his manners bland;
   Gay, handsome, brilliant, and, the truth to
      tell,

Pert and loquacious, as became his age ;
In short, well worthy of his holy cage.

III.

Dear to the sisters for his winning ways
　　Was gay Ver-Vert ; they kept him ever near,
And kindly taught him many a holy phrase,
　　Enforced with titbits from their daily cheer,
And loved him better — they would oft de-
　　clare —
Than any one, except their darling *Mère!*

IV.

Ah! ne'er was parrot happier than he ;
　　And happy was the lucky girl of whom
He asked — according as his whim might be —
　　The privilege at eve to share her room,
Where, perched upon the relics, he would sleep
Through the long night in slumber calm and
　　deep.

V.

At length, what joy to see!—the bird had grown,
  With good example, thoughtful and devout,
He said his prayers in such a nasal tone,
  His piety was quite beyond a doubt;
And some declared that soon, with proper
    teaching,
He'd rival the Superior at preaching!

VI.

If any laughed to see his solemn ways,
  In curt rebuke, " *Orate!* " * he replied;
And when his zeal provoked a shower of praise,
  " *Deo sit laus!* " † the humble novice cried;
And many said they did n't mind confessing
His " *Pax sit tecum!* " ‡ brought a special bless-
    ing.

* Pray !   † Praise be to God.
  ‡ Peace be with you.

VII.

Such wondrous talents, though awhile concealed,
　　Could not be kept in secrecy forever;
Some babbling nun the precious truth revealed,
　　And all the town must see a bird so clever;
Until at last so wide the wonder grew,
'T was fairly bruited all the country through.

VIII.

And so it fell, by most unlucky chance,
　　A distant city of the parrot heard;
The story reached some sister-nuns at Nantz,
　　Who fain themselves would see this precious
　　　　bird
Whose zeal and learning had sufficed to draw
On blest Nevers such honor and *éclat.*

IX.

What could they do? — well, here is what they
　　did,
　　To the good Abbess presently there went

A friendly note, in which the writers bid

    A thousand blessings hasten their descent

Upon her honored house, — and would she please

To grant a favor asked upon their knees?

X.

'T was only this, that she would deign to lend

    For a brief space that charming parroquet;

They hoped the bold request might not offend

    Her ladyship, but then they fain would get

Such proof as only he could well advance

To silence certain sceptic nuns of Nantz.

XI.

The letter came to hand, and such a storm

    Of pious wrath was never heard before;

The mildest sister waxed exceeding warm, —

    " *Perdre Ver-Vert! O ciel! plutôt la mort!* "

They all broke forth in one terrific cry,

What? — lose their darling? — they would

      rather die!

XII.

But, on reflection, it was reckoned best
  To take the matter into grave debate,
And put the question fairly to the test
  (Which seemed, indeed, a nice affair of state)
If they should lend their precious pet or not;
And so they held a session, long and hot.

XIII.

The sisters all with one accord express
  Their disapproval in a noisy " No! "
The graver dame — who loved the parrot less —
  Declared, Perhaps 't were best to let him go;
Refusal was ungracious, and, indeed,
An ugly quarrel might suffice to breed!

XIV.

Vain was the clamor of the younger set;
  " Just fifteen days and not a moment more
(Mamma decided) we will lend our pet;
  Of course his absence we shall all deplore,

But then, remember, he is only lent
For two short weeks," — and off the parrot
   went !

XV.

In the same bark that bore the bird away
 Were several Gascons and a vulgar nurse,
Besides two Cyprian ladies ; sooth to say,
 Ver-Vert's companions could n't have been
   worse.
Small profit such a youth might hope to gain
From wretches so licentious and profane.

XVI.

Their manners struck him as extremely queer ;
 Such oaths and curses he had never heard
As now in volleys stunned his saintly ear ;
 Although he did n't understand a word,
Their conversation seemed improper, very,
To one brought up within a monastery.

XVII.

For his, remember, was a Christian tongue
    Unskilled in aught save pious prose or verse
By his good sisters daily said or sung ;
    And now to hear the Gascons and the nurse
Go on in such a roaring, ribald way,
He knew not what to think, nor what to say.

XVIII.

And so he mused in silence ; till at last
    The nurse reproached him for a sullen fool,
And poured upon him a terrific blast
    Of questions, such as, where he 'd been to
        school.?
And was he used to travelling about ?
And did his mother know that he was out ?

XIX.

" *Ave Maria !* " * said the parrot, — vexed
    By so much banter into sudden speech, —

        * Hail Mary.

Whereat all laughed to hear the holy text,
  And cried, "By Jove! the chap is going to
    preach!"
" Come," they exclaimed, "let's have a song
    instead."
" *Cantate Domino!*"* the parrot said.

XX.

At this reply they laughed so loud and long
  That poor Ver-Vert was fairly stricken
    dumb.
In vain they teased him for a merry song;
  Abashed by ridicule and quite o'ercome
With virulent abuse, the wretched bird
For two whole days refused to speak a word!

XXI.

Meanwhile he listened to their vile discourse
  In deep disgust; but still the stranger
    thought

* Let us sing unto the Lord.

Their slang surpassed in freedom, pith and force
  The purer language which the missal taught,
And seemed, besides, an easier tongue to speak
Than prayer-book Latin or monastic Greek.

XXII.

In short, to tell the melancholy truth,
  Before the boat had reached its destined
    shore
He who embarked a pure, ingenuous youth
  Had grown a profligate, and cursed and
    swore
Such dreadful oaths as e'en the Gascons heard
With shame, and said, "The Devil's in the
  bird!"

XXIII.

At length, the vessel has arrived in port,
  And half the sisterhood are waiting there
To greet their guest, and safely to escort
  To their own house the wonderful Ver-
    Vert, —

The precious parrot whom their fancies paint
Crowned with a halo like a very Saint!

*

XXIV.

Great was the clamor when their eyes beheld
 The charming stranger in the emerald coat;
" Ver-Vert indeed ! " — his very hue compelled
 A shout of praise that reached the highest note.
" And then such eyes ! — and such a graceful
  walk !
And soon, — what rapture! — we shall hear
  him talk ! "

XXV.

At length — the Abbess in a nasal chant,
 (Intended, doubtless, for a pretty speech,)
Showered him with thanks that he had deigned
  to grant
 His worthy presence there, and to beseech
His benediction in such gracious terms
As might befit the sinfullest of worms.

XXVI.

Alas! for youthful piety; the bird,
    Still thinking o'er the lessons latest learned,
For a full minute answered not a word,
    And then, as if to show much he spurned
The early teachings of his holy school,
He merely muttered, " Curse the silly fool !"

XXVII.

The lady, startled at the queer remark,
    Could not but think that she had heard
        amiss;
And so began to speak again, — but hark!
    What diabolic dialect is this ? —
Such language for a saint was most improper,
Each word an oath, and every oath a whopper !

XXVIII.

Parblieu! Morblieu! and every azure curse
    To pious people strictly disallowed,

Including others that were vastly worse,

    Came rattling forth on the astonished crowd

In such a storm, that one might well compare

The dreadful volley to a *"feu d'enfer!"*

XXIX.

All stood aghast in horror and dismay;

    Some cried, " For shame ! is that the way
        they teach

Their pupils at *Nevers?*"   Some ran away,

    Rending the welkin with a piercing screech ;

Some stopt their ears for modesty ; and some

(Though shocked) stood waiting something
        worse to come !

XXX.

In brief, the dame, replete with holy rage

    At being thus insulted and disgraced,

Shut up the hateful parrot in his cage,

    And sent him back with all convenient haste

And this indignant note: — " In time to come
Be pleased to keep your precious prize at
  home ! "

XXXI.

When to *Nevers* the wicked wanderer came,
  All were delighted at his quick return ;
But who can paint their sorrow and their shame
  When the sad truth the gentle sisters learn,
That he who left them, chanting pious verses,
Now greets his friends with horrid oaths and
  curses !

XXXII.

'T is said that after many bitter days
  In wholesome solitude and penance passed,
Ver-Vert grew meek, reformed his wicked
  ways,
  And died a hopeful penitent at last.
The moral of my story is n't deep : —
" Young folks, beware what company you
  keep ! "

THE PUZZLED CENSUS-TAKER.

" GOT any boys ? " the Marshal said
  To a lady from over the Rhine ;
And the lady shook her flaxen head,
  And civilly answered, " *Nein !* " *

" Got any girls ? " the Marshal said
  To the lady from over the Rhine ;
And again the lady shook her head,
  And civilly answered, " *Nein !* "

" But some are dead ? " the Marshal said
  To the lady from over the Rhine ;
And again the lady shook her head,
  And civilly answered, " *Nein !* "

 * *Nein,* pronounced *nine,* is the German for " *No.* "

" Husband of course ? " the Marshal said
    To the lady from over the Rhine ;
And again she shook her flaxen head,
    And civilly answered, " *Nein!* "

" The d——l you have ! " the Marshal said
    To the lady from over the Rhine ;
And again she shook her flaxen head,
    And civilly answered, " *Nein!* "

" Now what do you mean by shaking your head,
    And always answering, ' *Nine* ' ? "
" *Ich kann nicht Englisch!* " civilly said
    The lady from over the Rhine ! "

EGO ET ECHO.

A PHANTASY.

I.

I ASKED of Echo, 't other day,
  (Whose words are few and often funny,)
What to a novice she could say
  Of courtship, love and matrimony?
  Quoth Echo, plainly: — " *Matter-o'-money!* "

II.

Whom should I marry? — should it be
  A dashing damsel, gay and pert, —
A pattern of inconstancy;
  Or selfish, mercenary flirt?
  Quoth Echo, sharply: — " *Nary flirt!* "

III.

What if — aweary of the strife
 That long has lured the dear deceiver —
She promise to amend her life,
 And sin no more, can I believe her?
 Quoth Echo, very promptly : — *"Leave her!"*

IV.

But if some maiden with a heart,
 On me should venture to bestow it:
Pray, should I act the wiser part
 To take the treasure ; or forego it?
 Quoth Echo, with decision : — *" Go it!"*

V.

Suppose a billet-doux, (in rhyme,)
 As warm as if Catullus penned it,
Declare her beauty so sublime
 That Cytherea's can't transcend it, —
 Quoth Echo, very clearly : — *" Send it!"*

VI.

But what if, seemingly afraid
   To bind her fate in Hymen's fetter,
She vow she means to die a maid, —
   In answer to my loving letter?
   Quoth Echo, rather coolly : — " *Let her !* "

VII.

What if, in spite of her disdain,
   I find my heart entwined about
With Cupid's dear delicious chain,
   So closely that I can't get out ?
   Quoth Echo, laughingly : — " *Get out !* "

VIII.

But if some maid with beauty blest ;
   As pure and fair as Heaven can make her,
Will share my labor and my rest,
   Till envious Death shall overtake her ? —
   Quoth Echo (*sotto voce*) : — " *Take her !* "

WOULD N'T YOU LIKE TO KNOW?

A MADRIGAL.

I.

I KNOW a girl with teeth of pearl,
   And shoulders white as snow;
     She lives, — ah! well,
     I must not tell, —
Would n't you like to know?

II.

Her sunny hair is wondrous fair,
   And wavy in its flow;
     Who made it less
     One little tress, —
Would n't you like to know?

III.

Her eyes are blue (celestial hue !)
And dazzling in their glow ;
 On whom they beam
 With melting gleam, —
Would n't you like to know ?

IV.

Her lips are red and finely wed,
Like roses ere they blow ;
 What lover sips
 Those dewy lips, — ·
Would n't you like to know ?

V.

Her fingers are like lilies fair
When lilies fairest grow ;
 Whose hand they press
 With fond caress, —
Would n't you like to know ?

VI.

Her foot is small, and has a fall
Like snowflakes on the snow ;
    And where it goes
    Beneath the rose, —
Would n't you like to know ?

VII.

She has a name, the sweetest name
That language can bestow ;
    'T would break the spell
    If I should tell, —
Would n't you like to know ?

THE COQUETTE.

A PORTRAIT.

" YOU 're clever at drawing, I own,"
    Said my beautiful cousin Lisette,
As we sat by the window alone,
    " But say, can you paint a Coquette? "

" She 's painted already," quoth I;
    " Nay, nay! " said the laughing Lisette,
" Now none of your joking, — but try
    And paint me a thorough Coquette."

" Well, cousin," at once I began
    In the ear of the eager Lisette,
" I 'll paint you as well as I can
    That wonderful thing, a Coquette.

9 *

She wears a most beautiful face,
   (Of course! — said the pretty Lisette,)
And is n't deficient in grace,
   Or else she were not a Coquette.

And then she is daintily made
   (A smile from the dainty Lisette)
By people expert in the trade
   Of forming a proper Coquette.

She's the winningest ways with the beaux,
   (Go on! — said the winning Lisette,)
But there is n't a man of them knows
   The mind of the fickle Coquette!

She knows how to weep and to sigh,
   (A sigh from the tender Lisette,)
But her weeping is all in my eye, —
   Not that of the cunning Coquette!

In short, she's a creature of art, .
  (O hush! — said the frowning Lisette,)
With merely the ghost of a heart, —
  Enough for a thorough Coquette.

And yet I could easily prove
  (Now don't! — said the angry Lisette,)
The lady is always in love, —
  In love with herself, — the Coquette!

There, — do not be angry! — you know,
  My dear little cousin Lisette,
You told me a moment ago
  To paint *you* — a thorough Coquette!"

THE LITTLE MAID AND THE LAWYER.

A SONG.

I.

THEY say, little maid, quoth Lawyer Brown,
I 'm the cleverest man in all the town.
Heigh-ho ! — says she,
What 's that to me ?
But they say, little maid, quoth Lawyer Brown,
You 're the prettiest girl in all the town !
Says she, If they do,
What 's that to you ?

II.

They say, little maid, quoth Lawyer Brown,
I 'm the richest man in all the town.
Heigh-ho ! — says she,
What 's that to me ?

But they say, little maid, quoth Lawyer Brown,
You ought to be dressed in a finer gown!
  Says she, If they do,
  What's that to you?

III.

They say, little maid, quoth Lawyer Brown,
That Johnny Hodge is an awkward clown.
  Heigh-ho! — says she,
  What's that to me?
But they say, little maid, the lawyer said,
That you and Johnny are going to wed!
  Says she, If we do,
  What's that to you?

TO MY LOVE.

Da me basia. CATULLUS.

I.

KISS me softly and speak to me low;
  Malice has ever a vigilant ear;
What if Malice were lurking near?
    Kiss me, dear!
Kiss me softly and speak to me low.

II.

Kiss me softly and speak to me low;
  Envy too has a watchful ear;
What if Envy should chance to hear?
    Kiss me, dear!
Kiss me softly and speak to me low.

III.

Kiss me softly and speak to me low;

  Trust me, darling, the time is near

  When lovers may love with never a fear;

    Kiss me, dear!

Kiss me softly and speak to me low.

·ROBIN MERRYMAN.

(Imitated from Béranger's " Roger Bontemps.")

I.

BY way of good example
  To all the gloomy clan,
There came into existence
  Good Robin Merryman.
To laugh at those who grumble,
  And be jolly as he can, —
O that 's the only system
  Of Robin Merryman!

II.

A hat so very ancient
  It might have covered Moses,

Adorned, on great occasions,
    With ivy-leaves or roses;
A coat the very coarsest
    Since tailoring began, —
O that's the gay apparel
    Of Robin Merryman!

III.

Within his cottage Robin
    With joyful eye regards
A table and a bedstead,
    A flute, a pack of cards,
A chest — with nothing in it, —
    An earthen water-can, —
O these are all the riches
    Of Robin Merryman!

IV.

To teach the village children
    The funniest kind of plays;

N

To tell a clever story ;
    To dance on holidays ;
To puzzle through the almanac ;
    A merry song to scan, —
O that is all the learning
    Of Robin Merryman !

v.

To drink his mug of cider,
    And never sigh for wine ;
To look at courtly ladies,
    Yet think his *Mag* divine ;
To take the good that 's going,
    Content with Nature's plan, —
O that is the philosophy
    'Of Robin Merryman !

vi.

To say, " O Gracious Father !
    Excuse my merry pranks ;

For all Thy loving-kindness
   I give Thee hearty thanks;
And may I still be jolly
   Through life's remaining span," —
O that's the style of praying
   With Robin Merryman!

VII.

Now, all ye wretched mortals
   . Aspiring to be rich;
And ye whose gilded coaches
   Have tumbled in the ditch;
Leave off your silly whining,
   Adopt a wiser plan;
Go follow the example
   Of Robin Merryman!

THE MERRY MONARCH.

(Imitated from Béranger's " Le Roi d'Yvetot.")

I.

IN Normandy there reigned a king,
  (I 've quite forgot his name,)
Who led a jolly sort of life,
  And did n't care for fame.
A nightcap was his crown of state,
Which Jenny placed upon his pate :
    Ha ! ha ! — laugh and sing :
    O was n't he a funny king ?

II.

He ate his meals, like other folk,
  Slept soundly and secure,

And on a donkey every year
  He made his royal tour ;
A little dog — it was his whim —
Was body-guard enough for him :
    Ha ! ha ! — laugh and sing :
    O was n't he a funny king ?

III.

A single foible he confessed, —
  A tendency to drink ;
But kings who heed their subjects' need,
  Should mind their own, I think ;
And thus it was his tax he got, —
For every cask an extra pot : - ·
    Ha ! ha ! — laugh and sing :
    O was n't he a funny king ?

IV.

The lasses loved this worthy king ;
  And many a merry youth

Would hail his majesty as " Sire,"
    And often spoke the truth.
He viewed his troops in goodly ranks,
But still their cartridges were blanks.
      Ha! ha! — laugh and sing:
      O was n't he a funny king?

v.

He never stole his neighbors' land
    To magnify his realm;
But steered his little ship of state
    With honor at the helm;
And when at last the king was dead,
No wonder all the people said: —
      " Ah! ah! — weep and sing:
      O was n't he a noble king?"

THE HUNTER AND THE MILKMAID.

(Imitated from Béranger's "Le Chasseur et la Laitière.")

I.

THE lark is singing her matin lay,
  O come with me, fair maiden, I pray;
Sweet, O sweet is the morning hour,
And sweeter still is yon ivied bower;
Wreaths of roses I 'll twine for thee,
O come, fair maiden, along with me!
     Ah! Sir Hunter, my mother is near;
     I really must n't be loitering here!

II.

Thy mother, fair maiden, is far away,
And never will listen a word we say;

I 'll sing thee a song that ladies sing
In royal castles to please the king;
A wondrous song whose magical charm
Will keep the singer from every harm.

> Fie! Sir Hunter, — a fig for your song;
> Good by! — for I must be going along!

III.

Ah! well, — if singing will not prevail,
I 'll tell thee, then, a terrible tale;
'T is all about a Baron so bold,
Huge and swart, and ugly and old,
Who saw the ghost of his murdered wife;
A pleasant story, upon my life!

> Ah! Sir Hunter, the story is flat;
> *I* know one worth a dozen of that.

IV.

I 'll teach thee, then, a curious prayer
Of wondrous power the wolf to scare,

And frighten the witch that hovers nigh
To blight the young with her evil eye;
O guard, fair maiden, thy beauty well,
A fearful thing is her wicked spell!

 O, I can read my missal, you know;
 Good by! Sir Hunter,— for I must go!

v.

Nay, tarry a moment, my charming girl;
Here is a jewel of gold and pearl;
A beautiful cross it is, I ween,
As ever on beauty's breast was seen:
There 's nothing at all but love to pay;
Take it, and wear it, but only stay!

 Ah! Sir Hunter, what excellent taste!
 I 'm not — in such — particular — haste!

10

SONNETS.

PAN IMMORTAL.

WHO weeps the death of Pan? Pan is
   not dead,
 But loves the shepherds still; * still leads the
  fauns
 In merry dances o'er the grassy lawns,
To his own pipes; as erst in Greece he led
The sylvan games, what time the god pursued
 The beauteous Dryopè. The Naiads still
 Haunt the green marge of every mountain rill;
The Dryads sport in every leafy wood;
Pan cannot die till Nature's self decease!
 Full oft the reverent worshipper descries
 His ruddy face and mischief-glancing eyes

---

* Pan curat oves, oviumque magistros. — VIRGIL.

Beneath the branches of old forest-trees
  That tower remote from steps of worldly men,
  Or hears his laugh far echoing down the glen!

THE VICTIM.

A GALLIC bard the touching tale has told
  How once — the customary dower to save —
  A sordid sire his only daughter gave
To a rich suitor, ugly, base, and old.
The mother too, such mothers there have been,
  With equal pleasure heard the formal vow,
  " With all my worldly goods I thee endow,"
And gave the bargain an approving grin.
Then, to the girl, who stood with drooping head,
  The pallid image of a wretch forlorn,
  Mourning the hapless hour when she was born,
The Priest said, " Agnes, wilt thou this man
    wed ? "

"Of this my marriage, holy man," said she,
"Thou art the first to say a word to me!"

TO SPRING.

"O VER PURPUREUM!"—Violet-colored Spring!
  Perhaps, good poet, in *your* vernal days
  The simple truth might justify the phrase;
But now, dear Virgil, there is no such thing!
Perhaps, indeed, in your Italian clime,
  Where o'er the year, if fair report be true,
  Four seasons roll, instead of barely *two*,
There still may be a verdant vernal time;
But *here*, on these our chilly Northern shores,
  Where April gleams with January's snows,—
  Not e'en a violet buds; and nothing "blows,"
Save blustering Boreas,— dreariest of bores.
O ver purpureum! where the Spring discloses
Her brightest purple on our lips and noses!

TO MY WIFE ON HER BIRTHDAY.

WHAT! ——ty years? — I never could have
    guessed it
  By any token writ upon your brow,   '
  Or other test of Time, — had you not now,
Just to surprise me, foolishly confessed it.
Well, — on your word, of course, I must receive
    it ;
  Although (to say the truth) it is, indeed,
  As proselytes sometimes accept a creed,
While in their hearts they really don't believe it!
While all around is changed, no change appears
  My darling Sophie, to these eyes of mine,
  In aught of thee that I have deemed divine,
To mark the number of the vanished years, —
  The kindly years that on that face of thine
  Have spent their life, and, " dying, made no
    sign ! "

THE DILEMMA.

Two fashionable women, rather gay
   Than wise, were bosom friends for many a
      year,
   And called each other darling, duck and
      dear,
As lovers do, — till, one unlucky day,
The younger, falling into sad disgrace,
   (An old suspicion blackening into proof,)
   Her cautious crony coldly kept aloof,
And, for a time, discreetly hid her face.
Meeting at last, the injured lady cries,
   " Is this the way you cherish and defend
   The wounded honor of your dearest friend ? "
" Of course I knew," the timid dame replies,
   " The tale was false, — but then what could I
      do ? —
   I have n't character enough for two ! "

THE PARVENU'S OPINION.

Novus, whose silly claim to "high position"
   Is genuine, if wealth can make it true ;
A youth whose stock — petrolean, not patri-
     cian —
   Shines none the less for being fresh and
     new, —
Standing before a flaming placard sees,
   Announcing thus the lecture of the night,
By Everett, — "The Age of Pericles!"
   Novus, half doubting if he reads aright,
Repeats the words (soliloquizing loud)
   " *The Age of Pericles!* — I wonder now
Why such a theme should gather all this crowd
   That throngs the door with such a mighty
     row ;
There is n't one among 'em, I 'll engage,
Who cares a fig about the fellow's age!"

THE GRATEFUL PREACHER.

A STROLLING preacher, " once upon a time,"
   Addressed a congregation rather slim
In numbers, — yet his subject was sublime,
   ('T was " Charity,") sonorous was the hymn ;
Fervent the prayer ; and though the house was
      small,
   He pounded lustily the Sacred Word,
And preached an hour as loud as he could bawl,
   As one who meant the Gospel should be
      heard.
And now, hehold, the preacher's hat is sent
   Among the pews for customary pence,
But soon returns as empty as it went ! —
   Whereat — low bowing to the audience —
He said, " My preaching is not all in vain ;
Thank God! I've got my beaver back again! "

THE AMBITIOUS PAINTER.

A PAINTER once — 't was many years ago —
　　Gave public notice it was his intent
　　To change his style of art ; and that he meant
" Henceforth to paint like Michael Angelo ! "
The artist's scheme was sensible, no doubt,
　　But still his pictures, though he thought them
　　　　fine,
　　Remained so poor in color and design,
His plan seemed rather hard to carry out.
By every common amateur surpassed,
　　The people laughed, as well enough they
　　　　might,
　　To see the fellow, in ambition's spite,
Go on a wretched dauber to the last !
　　To rival Genius in her great inventions
　　Needs (that 's the moral) more than good
　　　　intentions !

EPIGRAMS.

THE EXPLANATION.

CHARLES, discoursing rather freely
    Of the unimportant part
Which (he said) our clever women
    Play in Science and in Art,
" Ah! — the sex you undervalue ";
    Cried his lovely cousin Jane.
" No, indeed! " responded Charley,
    " Pray allow me to explain;
Such a paragon is woman,
    That, you see, it *must* be true
She is always vastly better
    Than the best that she can do! "

A COMMON ALTERNATIVE.

"SAY, what's to be done with this window,
    dear Jack? —
The cold rushes through it at every crack."
    Quoth John, "I know little of carpenter-craft,
But I think, my dear wife, you will have to go
    through
The very same process that other folks do, —
    That is, you must *'list* or submit to the
    draught!"

NEVER TOO LATE TO MEND.

"HERE, wife," said Will, "I pray you devote
Just half a minute to mend this coat
    Which a nail has chanced to rend."
"'T is ten o'clock!" said his drowsy mate.
"I know," said Will, "it is rather late;
    But 't is 'never too late to mend'!"

A PLAIN CASE.

WHEN Tutor Thompson goes to bed,
That very moment, it is said,
The cautious man puts out the light,
And draws the curtain snug and tight.
You marvel much why this should be,
· But when his spouse you chance to see,
What seemed before a puzzling case
Is plain as — Mrs. Thompson's face!

AN EQUIVOCAL APOLOGY.

QUOTH Madam Bas-bleu, " I hear you have said
Intellectual women are always your dread ;
 Now tell me, dear sir, is it true ? "
" Why, yes," answered Tom, " very likely I may
Have made the remark, in a jocular way ;
 But then, on my honor, I did n't mean you ! "

A CANDID CANDIDATE.

WHEN Thomas was running (though sure to be
    beat)
In the annual race for the Governor's seat,
And a crusty old fellow remarked, to his face,
He was clearly too young for so lofty a place, —
" Perhaps so," said Tom ; " but consider a
    minute ;
The objection will cease by the time I am in it ! "

ON A DÉCOLLETÉ DRESS.

THAT " effects are the same from a similar
    cause,"
Is one of the famous Socratian laws
    Whose fallacy we may discover ;
For — quite in the teeth of the logical rule —
The style of apparel that keeps Emma cool,
    Just kindles a flame in her lover !

LUCUS A NON—

You 'll oft find in · books, rather ancient than
 recent,
A gap in the page marked with " *cetera desunt,*"
By which you may commonly take it for granted
The passage is wanting without being wanted ;
And may borrow, besides, a significant hint
That *desunt* means simply *not* decent to print !

NEMO REPENTE TURPISSIMUS.

BOB SAWYER to a man of law
Repeating once the Roman saw
" *Nemo repente* " and the rest,
Was answered thus, " Well, I protest,
However classic your quotation,
I do not see the application."
" 'T is plain enough," responded Sawyer :
" *It takes three years to make a lawyer !* "

CONJURGIUM NON CONJUGIUM.

DICK leads, it is known, with his vixenish wife,
In spite of their vows, such a turbulent life,
The social relation of Dick and his mate
Should surely be written The Conjurgal State!

TOO CANDID BY HALF.

As John and his wife were discoursing one day
Of their several faults, in a bantering way,
  Said she, " Though my *wit* you disparage,
I 'm sure, my dear husband, our friends will at-
    test
This much, at the least, that my *judgment* is
    best."
  Quoth John, " So they said at our mar-
    riage ! "

CHEAP ENOUGH.

THEY 've a saying in Italy, pointed and terse,
That a pretty girl's smiles are the tears of the
purse ;
" What matter ? " says Charley.   " Can dia-
monds be cheap ?
Let lovers be happy, though purses should
weep ! "

Cambridge : Stereotyped and Printed by Welch, Bigelow, & Co.

www.ingramcontent.com/pod-product-compliance
Lightning Source LLC
Chambersburg PA
CBHW030815020726
47499CB00006B/1924